THE UNTOLD TALE

OF

SHADY BADESSO

A NOVEL

Matt Micros

It is the things you least expect that hit you the hardest.

<u>*Also by Matt Micros*</u>

~Five Days~

~The Knights of Redemption~

~The Chameleon~

~The Greatest Mann in the World~

~Nick Nelson Was Here~

~The Music Box~

~Destinare~

*~Slow Drinkers, Giant Ballbags & Smelly
Bastards~*

TABLE OF CONTENTS

THE UNTOLD TALE OF SHADY BADESSO

For the real-life Casey Hutchinson, Steve Smith and John Carideo...

This book is a work of fiction.
No part of the contents relate to any real person or persons living or dead. No events depicted actually happened or are implied to have happened.

I ~Shady~

Shady Badesso arrived in Niantic, Connecticut from nowhere. With arms as thick and sturdy as PVC pipe, a back broader than a drive-in movie screen, and legs the size of a 75 year old oak tree, he looked like he was built from leftover parts at a hardware store, which was fitting because that's exactly where he worked. It was impossible to tell which of the above-mentioned features he inherited from his parents, because he never spoke of them. He was friendly, but had very few friends. If you googled him you would find absolutely NOTHING. If you were to ask anyone in town when and how they first met Shady, they likely wouldn't be able to recall. He had always just been there, or so it seemed. It was as if he had been dropped into the small, northern coastal Connecticut town from thin air.

***

Jeremy Hutchinson stood rather unsteadily atop the six-foot ladder as he attempted to shove a box of paint primer onto the top shelf in the back room of Clough's Hardware. The ladder was steadied at the bottom by Shady's strong hand.

"Remind me why I'm on this ladder again instead of you?" Jeremy asked.

"Because you're taller. And because that ladder wouldn't come close to holding my weight," Shady responded.

One quick glance was all it took to know he was right. Shady wasn't fat. He was solid. Like a large rectangle.

"Then why are we putting heavy boxes on the top shelf?" Jeremy followed up with.

"Because we don't sell much paint primer these days. Would you rather have to pull light bulbs down 5 times a day?"

"At this moment, yes," he answered before adding, "are you even holding this ladder??"

It began to wobble like a beer bottle during an earthquake. Jeremy looked down abruptly. "Shady?"

But Shady was nowhere to be found. The wobble quickly became a rocking motion and just as Jeremy started to fall, he reached out with one of his long arms and latched on to the shelf, swinging like a monkey in the wild. He let go when he was safely over the oversized recycle bin they used for their cardboard boxes and landed with a softer than expected thud into the middle of it.

"What are you doing?" Shady asked upon his return. "Stop screwing around. We've got work to do."

"You left me on a wobbling six-foot ladder holding a 40 pound box."

"Mrs. Mahoney needed help loading her groceries into her car."

"I could have killed myself."

"Mrs. Mahoney is 83. You'll live."

"I think I broke my arm," Jeremy moaned, rubbing it gently.

"Stop being so dramatic. Your arm is moving better than a windshield wiper. Now, up you go," Shady said, helping him to his feet.

Jeremy didn't argue, except to mumble something about his sister not being happy if Shady got her little brother killed, in part because he looked up to him, in part because he knew it wouldn't matter if he did argue, but mostly because his personality was such that he was too easy going to waste much time arguing. Jeremy was 26, never went to college, and had never left the town he grew up in except for a yearly pilgrimage to the casino about 20 minutes away. He worked to live, instead of the other way around. Jeremy lived with his sister and worked at the hardware store during the week, while working his way through most of the girls in town on the weekend. He would never be rich or famous, but had an easy charm about him that women were drawn to.

The bell on the storefront door rang, indicating someone had entered. Jeremy stuffed the last box onto the shelf before throwing himself backwards into Shady like the lead singer of a band crowd surfing at a concert. Shady didn't even flinch. Caught him with one arm and propped him back up.

"One of these days, you're going to do that and I'm going to let you fall," Shady warned.

"You already did that a few minutes ago," Jeremy reminded him.

They arrived at the front of the store and found a frail looking elderly man bundled from head to toe in seven layers of winter clothing.

"Mr. Meyers? Is that you under all those layers?" Shady asked.

"Yes, it is, Shady. It was a cold walk to town. Had to bundle up."

"You walked in? Something wrong with your car?"

"Car is fine. Other than being snowed in. The young man who has been shoveling me out the last few years is off in college, and it seems like young people don't want to make a quick 20 bucks anymore. So here I am, looking to buy a shovel so I can dig myself out."

Peter Meyers was in his 70's, not exactly frail, but not in peak condition either, although he would probably argue he was. He had lived a very independent life over the past 15 years ever since his wife died, and he was too proud to change now — even though he knew that day was coming sooner than later.

"Tell you what," Shady said, "Jump in my truck with me and we'll go get my snow blower. I'll have your car out of there in ten minutes flat."

"I don't want to put you out."

"You're not putting me out at all. I'll take care of it for you."

"I'll pay you," Mr. Meyers said.

"You don't need to pay me. All you need to do is whip me up a couple of six packs of your home crafted beer every couple of months."

"It's a deal."

"Jeremy. Lock up will you?"

"No problem," he answered. "Just make sure you're not late for dinner. You know how it makes my sister crazy."

"Am I ever?"

"Only always."

"Well, I won't be this time. What time's dinner and what are we eating?"

"6 o'clock sharp and I don't know about *we*, but I'm headed to the Horseshoe with Jenny. Figured I'd give you some alone time so you can *not* ask Casey out for the 1000th time."

"I'm working my way up to it."

"I've seen highway workers move faster than you."

"I'm pacing myself," Shady laughed. "Don't forget to lock the back door."

"We live in Niantic. Nothing ever happens here."

"There's a state prison ten minutes down the road."

"Yeah and I'm sure if someone broke out, they'd head straight to the local hardware store to pick up some light bulbs," Jeremy cracked.

"Or maybe a hacksaw. For some chains..." Shady pointed out with an emphasis on the second sentence.

"I guess when you put it that way."

"C'mon, Mr. Meyers, let's get you dug out."

While it was less than ten minutes to actually plow the driveway, Shady had neglected to take into account that it took three times as long to load the snow blower onto the back of his flatbed and drive across town to Mr. Meyers house. But he did it anyway and would continue to do it for the foreseeable future.

Shady pulled in front of Casey Hutchinson's house and knocked on the door at precisely 6:03. There was some shuffling inside before a woman of average height, who looked to be in her late 20's or early 30's, opened the door. She had shoulder length, wavy brown hair that was pulled up on top of her head, revealing a long, thin, neck that led to perhaps her greatest feature—her smile. Her brown eyes matched her hair, and while it was unusual to describe brown eyes as glistening, hers definitely glistened. She was wearing jeans, and she wore them well, with a loose-fitting navy, v- neck sweater.

"You're late," Casey said.

"You're stunning," Shady managed to force out as if he was a balloon just as the last gasp of air had been squeezed out of it.

"Did you steal that from Richard Gere in *Pretty Woman*?" she asked accusingly.

"Did it work?"

"No."

"Then yes."

She shook her head and stepped aside to let him enter.

II ~Casey~

Casey's home wasn't overly large, but it was beautifully decorated and immaculate. Every pot and oversized utensil in the kitchen had its own hook overhead and there wasn't a drop of grease on the stove top. Even the dish towels were color coordinated and spotless. Shady found that to be most impressive of all. Even the things used to clean other things were clean.

"So what are you cooking in this contraption over here?" Shady asked as he peered into it.

"By contraption I assume you mean the crockpot?"

"The crackpot?"

"CROCKpot. It's a slow cooker. And braised chicken with a pomegranate marinade is inside it. Can you stir it a little for me?" Casey asked as she pulled a half dozen, soft tortillas from the oven.

"Define a little," Shady answered. He would never be confused with Bobby Flay. "And you have broken the golden rule of food."

"Three or four times is enough. And what rule is that?"

"Never mix salty foods with sweet ones."

"I've never heard of that rule," she said.

"It's my rule. People who put pear vinaigrette with raisins on their salad should be charged with crimes against humanity."

"Interesting," Casey responded as she deftly hid the pear vinaigrette behind her back and slid it back onto a shelf in the refrigerator.

"You wouldn't put maple syrup on your steak."

"What about chocolate or yogurt covered pretzels?" she asked.

"Those people should be shot," Shady continued.

"That seems a bit harsh," Casey answered as she pulled another bottle out. "*Newman's Own Olive Oil & Vinegar* dressing."

"My favorite," Shady answered. "Partly because Newman was my favorite actor. Partly because all the profits go to charity. But mainly because it doesn't break the rule."

"Speaking of rules, did you watch the hearing today?"

"We had it on in the background," Shady answered as he helped her carry the food into the dining room.

"What did you think?"

"You don't want to know what I think."

"If I didn't want to know, I wouldn't have asked."

"I think the FBI has a serious credibility problem. The director breaks protocol during one investigation that undoubtedly influenced the election. He also leaked confidential information. And then his second in command is guilty at the very least of extremely poor judgement and the appearance of extreme bias towards the President."

"I don't understand how you can support the President with all the divisiveness he has created."

"I don't support the President. I support some of his policies. There's a difference."

"How is there a difference?"

"That's the problem with the system. It forces people to choose between the lesser of two evils. They may agree on some issues and not on others, but they need to decide which issues are most important and vote accordingly. For example, I agree with tightening the boarders and making people enter the country the correct way. I'd much rather have someone denied entrance while they are properly vetted, than risk harm to a US Citizen at the hands of an illegal alien."

"The number of people that actually happens to is minuscule."

"That may be, but even one person is too many. What's the worst thing that happens if someone is denied entry? Nothing. In cases of people seeking asylum, you can expedite the process for them and house them temporarily."

"What about other issues? Like the Supreme Court. Or same sex marriage. Equality in the workplace..."

"I believe too much time is wasted in a bogged down court system. People will be less inclined to sue if they know at the top it won't go anywhere. I believe in smaller government, lower taxes, less spending and term limits. But I also believe in people receiving equal pay for equal work, a person's right to marry the person they love, regardless of sex, and affordable healthcare for all by regulating the healthcare industry. And therein lies the problem. I agree with ideas on both sides, but disagree with ideas on both sides as well. There is nowhere for people like me to stand."

"I get that, but this President has been so...so...awful, I just don't see how you can support him."

"Again. I don't support him. I support a few of his ideas. And I think a lot of that divisiveness has been made worse by a media that was absent from journalism school the years they thought journalism. First rule is report the news. Don't be a part of it. I'm not interested in their opinion. I'm interested in facts."

"So you think our intelligence agencies have a credibility problem and our media is biased."

"Exactly,"   Shady   answered   while clinking wine glasses with Casey.

It was amazing that they could have two polar opposite viewpoints and yet share a meal as if they were talking about the Mets or a movie one of them had recently seen.

"Meanwhile, a womanizing, racist is the leader of the free world," Casey argued.

"He may be a womanizer and if so, I certainly don't support that, but he hasn't done a single thing that leads me to believe he's a racist."

"Charlottesville?"

"He didn't support the violence and he didn't support the right-wing extremists. He simply said he believes there were good people there on both sides. Referring to the people that wanted the statues to stay up out of a respect for history. Those were not the same people that were fighting. But they were in favor of the statues remaining."

"Insulting the parents of a slain soldier?"

"Can't really defend that other than to say I think the President is too thin skinned. When someone attacks him, he fights back, usually by saying something hurtful and spiteful. And that's just not how a President should act. But I'll say this. While I don't like the man personally from what I've seen, I do agree with some of his policies. There have been previous presidents that I didn't agree with a single thing they tried to enact, but I probably would have enjoyed having a beer with them. Which is worse? I don't know."

"You were right. I didn't want to know what you thought," Casey laughed.

"I told you. But here's the thing, and it's the reason I can tolerate our president. Have you ever read the book _The Knights of Redemption_?"

She shook her head that she hadn't.

"Well, it's kind of an adult version of _The Breakfast Club_. Anyway, it's the story of five guys arrested the same night and thrown in jail together for unrelated crimes. Each of them is deeply flawed in some respect. But each of them also has redeeming qualities. The main theme of the story is wondering how different the world would look if everyone was judged solely by the worst thing they'd ever done. Besides, as my father used to say, 'no matter how wonderful you are, there are only two times in your life where everyone will say only good things about you — your wedding and your funeral. And you'll only be around for one of them.'"

"Well, then our president is more fortunate than most since he's been married four times."

"You do make a good point," Shady nodded.

"I like it when you talk about your parents. You don't do it very often. When did they die?"

"They're not dead," he answered solemnly. "I just don't see them very often."

"They're alive?" Casey asked, stunned.

"Yeah."

"Where do they live?"

"Outside of Dallas where I grew up."

"I can't believe I didn't know your parents were alive. And I can't believe I haven't met them. Why don't you invite them up for a white Christmas?"

"It's complicated," Shady answered in a tone that indicated he didn't want to talk about it any longer.

"Movin on," Casey laughed. "So what did you really think of my cilantro salsa, pomegranate flavored chicken tortillas?" she asked.

"I think they were surprisingly excellent."

"Excellent enough to be an exception to your rule?"

"Don't get carried away."

Although occasionally infuriating, Casey was easy to converse with, and Shady had loved her from the moment they met. But she had sent out enough mixed signals over the years that he never felt comfortable acting on those feelings until he eventually reached a point where too much time had passed to even try.

But it didn't stop him from thinking about it.

III ~Lindsey~

Old Man Clough still came into the hardware store a couple of times a week even as he approached his 80th birthday. He thought he was helping, but the reality was his appearance actually created more work for Shady and Jeremy than it relieved, mainly because he never saw a problem he didn't try to fix. When he was younger, he was McGuyver before there was McGuyver. Word had it if you gave him a string, a pair of scissors and a match, he could build a car engine. As he grew older, his kindness continued, but he didn't quite have the skills any longer to match, so he offered out Shady as a substitute.

"Someone broke into the middle school last night and stole a bunch of their computers," Old Man Clough announced when Shady entered the store.

"Damnit!" Shady screamed with far more anguish than expected, pounding his fist into the counter for emphasis.

"Take it easy there, big fella," Jeremy said. "No one got hurt."

"I hate when people don't respect other people's property. Just because someone is struggling, that gives them the right to take from somebody else? How about getting a job?"

"You sound like a cop."

"It pisses me off," Shady answered, calming slightly.

"Well, I'm glad you feel that way," Old Man Clough said, "because then you won't mind that I volunteered you to go over there today and fix the door and lock."

"I'll do it, Earl," Jeremy offered, looking for a change of scenery.

"You? You'd end up locking yourself *in* the room," Shady said. "I'll take care of it."

At the time it was built a little more than 15 years ago, East Lyme Middle School, located in Niantic, was a state-of-the-art facility, until the population aged and people grew tired of paying for other people's kids' education, even though others had paid for theirs. It had more band aids than actual repairs or updates to the building, which made a break-in through rusting locks not surprising.

It would have taken Shady about 30 minutes on a normal day to change out an exterior bar lock and an interior handle lock, were it not for a long pair of legs that were attached to a blonde-haired woman whose skirt and blouse "skirted" the fine line between flattering and slutty. The top two buttons on her white top were unbuttoned, revealing ample, but not an over-abundance of cleavage if she turned a certain way or you had the right angle, so Shady spent the better part of the morning trying to find that right angle.

Lindsey Thompson taught Computer Science in what was called a "Kiva", a controversial educational system that attempted to make larger schools feel smaller by splitting them into groups of 70 to 80 students that rotated through four adjoining classrooms. Critics of the system didn't like it because the kids rarely had any interaction with students outside of their Kiva, but the 5th grade boys in Miss Thompson's class couldn't have cared less about that. Lindsey was in her early 30's, with a seductively devilish smile and pools of crystal clear blue eyes that you felt like you could swim in. She had taught there for only a few months, during which time the participation amongst the fathers on parent-teacher night had increased by about 75%.

"You would have finished those locks a lot sooner if you weren't staring at my ass all morning," were the first words she ever spoke to Shady after the last of her students had filed out for lunch.

"I wasn't staring..." he started before his voice trailed off in a futile effort to defend himself, "but even if I had been, how would you know unless you have eyes in the back of your head?"

"There's this little thing called window reflection," she answered as Shady leaned sideways to see if that was even possible.

"If I break something else, do you get to come back tomorrow?" she asked playfully, touching him gently on the shoulder as she walked past.

If Shady didn't believe in love at first sight, he definitely believed in lust at first sight after meeting her. There was something about this woman that made it impossible to take his eyes off of her. She even knew how to walk, her hips swinging seductively with every step. And when she touched him on the shoulder....good lord.

IV ~Captain Adventurous~

Jeremy finished stacking the last of the boxes of car wax, pyramid-style next to the counter.

"You see the Cowboys game last night?"

"Of course I did," Shady answered.

"What were they thinking rushing to the line for the 4th and 1, instead of challenging the spot first?"

"That I don't know. It was not smart."

"Then they get the ball back up two scores and on 3rd down, they throw it instead of running it and making the Skins burn their last timeout."

"That I can understand. There was about three and a half minutes left at that point. If they got the first down, the game was over. If they missed either by running or passing, the Skins would have needed to score AND get the onside kick to win. The extra timeout wouldn't have affected anything as long as the Cowboys recovered the ball," Shady explained.

"You should be a coach."

"I used to be. A long time ago in a galaxy far, far away."

The bell rang over the door and Lindsey Thompson entered, flipping the long curls of her hair in the air after taking off the knit-hat she had been wearing.

"It's really cold out there," she said. And then, upon spotting Shady, added with a smile, "Well, hello there."

Jeremy looked around to see if she was talking to him. "Hi," he stammered.

"She was talking to me," Shady answered.

"Came into town to pick up some groceries and thought the hardware store might be the place to point me in the right direction. My landlord has this old pickup truck that he said I could use if I can get it running. Do you know of anyone who might be able to take a look at it?"

"Chuck's Garage is right down the street. He'll come out--" Jeremy said before being interrupted by Shady.

"Chuck doesn't do house calls," Shady corrected. "Yes, he does," Jeremy persisted.

"He used to. But now he just sends a tow truck out to bring it to the shop and he'll charge you for that. I'm pretty good with cars. I'll have a look if you like," Shady said as he pushed past Jeremy with the force of a wrecking ball. He didn't intend to, but his sheer size and strength sent Jeremy flying ass over tea cups into his car wax display.

Lindsey gasped and covered her mouth with her hand to stifle a laugh.

"What is wrong with you?" Shady admonished. "You can't even stay on your feet?"

"Thank you," she answered with a soft laugh. "When would be a good time for you?"

"Now is as good a time as any. I'll be back in an hour or so," Shady said as Jeremy dusted himself off and began restacking the boxes.

***

Lindsey's rented home was a small and clean ranch-style house set back from the road about five minutes outside of town. It was exactly what you would expect a middle school teacher's house to look like. Potted flowers adorned both sides of the front door. The yard was neat with a mixture of wild grass and what had been bright flowers before fall had turned to winter and everything was cut back for a spring that was still a few months away. There was a stray leaf or two that had wandered into the yard from the plentiful trees that surrounded the property. They looked a bit out of place sitting atop the six inches of snow, as if they had gotten lost on their way to the ground, landing a bit later than the rest.

Parked in the turnabout at the top of the driveway was a cherry red, Chevy pickup truck that appeared to be circa 1995. It wasn't in bad shape. No rust. No real dents. It wasn't fancy like the modern trucks of the day, but it was comfortable and functional. It just wouldn't start.

"When you try to start it, does it click or is it just completely dead?" Shady asked as he popped the hood on the 8 cylinder 400+ horsepower engine.

"The interior lights come on and it clicks. At times it sounds like it might turn over, but then doesn't," she answered, sounding a bit more car savvy than perhaps Shady had expected.

"Sounds like a loose distributor cap. If they're cracked or loose, moisture can get in there, which makes it difficult to turn over. Yup, that's what it is," he confirmed as he tinkered under the hood. He walked back to his own truck, a similar one about ten years newer and grabbed a drill and a couple of long screws out of the tool box in the flat bed. "It doesn't appear to be cracked," he explained, "so if I drill it nice and tight, it should seal it up."

A couple of pops from the drill gun later and Shady motioned for her to try and start it. It turned over on the first try with a huge roar followed by a little rattle from the nearly 25 year old truck that had more than 200,000 miles on it.

"Thank   you!"   Lindsey   screamed enthusiastically over the roar.

"No problem."

"So what should we do now?" she asked with a smile.

"I don't know about *we*, but I've got to get back to the store. Some of us work on Saturdays."

"I'm sure your partner can handle it."

"My partner can barely stay on his feet as you saw. But even if he could, it's called being responsible."

"Cluck, cluck cluck. Cluck-awwwwkk!!!" Lindsey clucked like a chicken. She was taunting him now. He shook his head, refusing to be goaded into doing something he knew he shouldn't do. Until he was.

"Where are we going?" Shady finally grumbled.

"Get in," she answered as she slid behind the seat of the pickup truck.

Shady texted Jeremy, "Stuck here for a while. Please close up and don't forget to lock the back door."

"*You dirty bastard,*" was Jeremy's three-word response.

A few minutes later, Lindsey pulled into the nearly vacant lot at Hole-in-the-Wall Beach, a stone's throw from the Niantic Boardwalk, the mile long stretch that ran parallel to the Long Island Sound. The lone other car in the lot belonged to a fisherman, who had just finished packing up his SUV before driving away.

"What are we doing here?" Shady asked.

"Isn't it beautiful?" she responded.

"It would be beautiful. In August. But it's December."

"C'mon. We're going swimming," she answered, grabbing a towel from inside the truck.

"I don't know about you, but 'we' are doing no such thing."

"Don't be such a baby," she admonished.

"Are you high? It's 25 degrees out."

"I have to say I'm a bit disappointed that a man named 'Shady' isn't a bit more adventurous."

"Give me one good reason why I would want to plunge fully clothed into freezing cold water?"

"We're not going in fully clothed," she answered matter-of-factly before adding, "and you'll get to see me naked. Isn't that reason enough?"

With that, she began peeling off her clothes, each layer more enticing than the one before it. She smiled when she was done and began sprinting toward the Sound. Shady took a quick look at his surroundings to see if anyone else was in view. He seemed to be doing the mental calculus of weighing the benefits of skinny dipping with Lindsey, versus most likely catching pneumonia from the frigid Long Island Sound water, before taking off his clothes and running in to join her.

"Oh....my....GOD!" Shady screamed when he reached her.

"Isn't it amazing?" she asked.

"That's not the word that comes to mind. Can we get out now?" he pleaded.

"Yup!" she laughed as she climbed out of the water and raced for the truck.

He wasn't far behind her. "I'm so cold I can't feel my skin," Shady moaned.

"C'mere," Lindsey said as she pulled him up against her, skin on skin, and wrapped the towel and her arms around them both. "Body heat. Is that better?"

"It's not worse," he admitted.

"It's starting to feel like you're getting warmer," she said with a sly smile.

"Probably still need a few more minutes."

She grabbed his clothes and tossed them into the cab of the truck. "Maybe we should try to drive home like this." She pushed him onto the driver's seat and climbed on top of him.

"I'm not so sure this will be very easy," he said.

"I thought you were adventurous," she whispered in his ear before starting to softly kiss his neck.

V ~The Big Show~

*T*he warm body pressed against him and the hot breath on the back of his neck made Shady feel a bit claustrophobic. He never understood why women felt the need to lie right next to you when they had an entire bed to sleep on. And in his next breath he wondered the proper etiquette of how long he needed to lie in the bed before bolting for the door and going home to get some real sleep. It had been a while since he found himself in this position.

He rolled over slowly and found the chestnut colored eyes of a 95 pound Black Labrador Retriever staring back at him, his head resting on his pillow like a human. The dog yawned and stretched, placing a paw directly on Shady's shoulder.

"Who are you?" Shady asked, half expecting the dog to answer in English.

"That's The Big Show," Lindsey answered, awake now.

"After the wrestler?"

"Yup. He's big and strong like him."

"I don't recall seeing him last night.   And I

think I would have remembered."

"Big Show likes to go on a walkabout at night. He comes back when he's ready and lets himself in by pushing down on the handle and pulling it open."

"Does he know how to close the door behind himself as well?"

"That part is a work in progress," she answered.

"Aren't you worried about a bear or some other animal getting into the house?"

"Nah. All the animals are afraid of Big Show. He's the king of the jungle. Aren't you boy?" she said while playfully rubbing his belly.

"Ok if I flip on the TV for a few minutes?" Shady asked. "Or should I ask The Big Show?"

"Rawfff!" Big Show responded.

"He says it's ok," Lindsey translated.

"Fox News?" Shady asked after turning it on. "I thought all teachers were died in the wool liberals?"

"I just watch that show Prison Breakout on it. Have you seen it?"

Shady shook his head no.

"They go to a different maximum security prison each week and ask a former inmate from there how they would break out if they had to. It shows the weaknesses of each prison."

"That doesn't sound very smart? Giving prisoners ideas on how to break out? They do have TV in jail."

"They don't air the episodes until after they've fixed the weaknesses."

"Seems a little risky to me. But anything for ratings I guess," he responded before changing the subject back. "You sure you're not a closet Politico?"

"Hell no. I haven't voted in years."

"And yet you're a teacher."

"I teach English. Writing. Reading. And occasionally, a little comprehension. I leave the three branches of government, number of Senators in the Senate, and number of people in the House to the history teachers."

"Executive. Legislative. Judicial. 100. And 435."

"Congratulations.   You just passed 8th grade US History."

"Do I get a gold star?"

"No. But what are you doing today?" she asked.

It was such a loaded question, he wasn't sure how to respond. If he said he was busy and she said she had tickets to the Rangers game at the Garden, he would have to walk back his answer like a Presidential candidate. If he said he was free and she asked him to lie in bed watching movies on the Hallmark Channel, he'd want to leap off a bridge. Why not just come out and ask your question? He supposed women did it that way on purpose to trap you.

In this game of social roulette, he pulled the trigger. "Nothing really," he answered slowly.

"Sunday is walk day for the Big Show. How'd you like to join us?"

He thought it over for a brief moment and looked at the dog's sad eyes that almost seemed to be begging him to come. "Why not?"

***

The woods behind Lindsey's house were expansive and surprisingly bright in spite of the tall trees. The Big Show ran out ahead in the path exploring, but was sure to circle back every few minutes to make sure they were ok.

"He's a good boy," Shady said. "Where'd you get him?"

"A friend of mine runs a lab rescue in town and asked me to foster him for a weekend while she took delivery of a few new dogs. I gave him back on that Sunday night and two days later he showed up at my door and let himself in. She lives five miles away. I figured anyone who would go to that much trouble just to see me, I had to keep. Watch this," she said. "Big Show!"

The giant lab came galloping back towards them like he was on the final turn of the Kentucky Derby.

"He's a tracking dog. I think he has some hound in him."

She handed her gloves to Shady.

"Hold him back and I'm going to go hide. In five minutes, rub these gloves in his face and then let him go. He'll find me."

Big Show seemed perfectly content to sit there and be pet by Shady, but after five minutes had passed, Shady did as he was told. Rubbed the gloves in the dog's face and turned him loose. Big Show took off into the woods with a purpose. In mere moments, Shady could barely see him in the distance. Big Show went right and left. Zig-zagging his way through the forest as Shady slowly caught up to him. The dog took off again, but then put on the brakes and stopped in his tracks. He slowly walked over to a stump next to a fallen tree and began to dig at the snow pile.

"Ok! Ok! You found me!" Lindsey laughed as she brushed the snow off and stood.

Shady had just caught up to them at that point.

Big Show was as proud as a peacock.

"And now you're soaking wet. But I guess you proved your point," Shady said.

"Yeah. I didn't think that one through very clearly. Probably should head back before I attempt to catch pneumonia for the second time in as many days."

"So what brought you to Connecticut in the first place?" Shady asked while they walked. "A guy?"

"Hell no," she answered defiantly in her trademark response. "You may not have noticed, but I'm a bit of a free spirit."

"You don't say?" Shady chuckled sarcastically.

"Yeah, I am. And I love experiencing different things. I've lived all over. Los Angeles. New York City. Arizona. Chicago. Even Kansas. That was for a guy. Never again. But I'd never gotten to experience a New England fall, so I thought I would. How bout you? Were you born and raised here?"

"I've been here so long it seems like it sometimes, but no. I was raised in Texas. Outside of Dallas."

"How'd you end up here then?" Lindsey asked, wrapping her arm around his and pulling him tight in an effort to warm up.

"One summer, I decided to travel the country. I visited landmarks, monuments, relatives and friends. On my way to Boston, I stopped for lunch in a small, coastal, Connecticut town and started talking to a guy that owned a hardware store. He needed some help, so I offered to help him. Figured it would be six months. 15 years later, I'm still here."

"You must really like it."

"I love that the people all know each other. I love that the social life all revolves around the local high school. And I love that whatever else is going on in the world, in Niantic, you can escape from it all."

"Sounds like as good a place as any."

"It can be."

"And yet you've never been married."

"How do you know that?" he asked.

"Just a hunch."

"I guess you could say I've spent quite a few years in the friend zone," Shady explained.

"It's a great place to visit, but no place to live," she responded.

"How bout you?"

"Almost was—once. But it didn't work out. He left me."

"I don't even know him, but I know he was stupid."

"Well, you see, I have this thing where I'm attracted to all the wrong guys."

"First step is recognizing the problem. Second step is fixing it."

"That's what I'm attempting to do," she laughed.

"So I'm the experiment? Not sure if I should be offended or glad that I'm not considered the 'wrong' guy."

"It's too early to tell if you're the wrong guy, but you seem pretty decent so far," she smiled.

VI ~The Christmas Ball~

The horse drawn carriage pulled up to the curb in front of Casey's house and Shady helped her into the carriage before he and Jeremy climbed in after her.

"I can't believe you agreed to ride to the party in a horse and buggy," Casey exclaimed excitedly. "That's so..."

"So..."

"So not you," she smiled.

"Well, I'm trying to get into the spirit of the season," Shady answered.

The Annual Christmas Ball was as old as Niantic, an elegant affair for the entire town filled with food, drinks, music and dancing. It was always held at a farmhouse on the edge of town, close enough that it was easy to get to, but just far enough away from the beaten path so as not to disturb the few curmudgeons who decided not to attend.

The horse made its way up the gravel driveway, white lights adorning the archway at the entrance; the horse's hoof prints and the carriage wheels following the path of the dozens that had come before them, while snowflakes as large as softballs softly floated to earth glistening in the lights.

Two rows of carolers on the front lawn sang *White Christmas.* The men were dressed in overcoats and top hats while the women wore long hoop dresses with shawls and a hat. One of the men was the Mayor.

"Gotta love a small town," Shady said. "It's the only place where you'll see the Mayor singing alongside the manager of Shop Rite and the high school janitor."

"That's exactly what I love about it," Casey gushed.

After a few more moments, the carolers in the front faded away and music could be heard from beneath the giant white tent in the backyard. White linen table cloths covered each table and were visible through the clear plastic sides of the tent that sealed it tightly. A dance floor had a dozen or so couples on it. Waiters in white gloves brought around trays of hor'devoures. A buffet was set up on both sides of the room.

They stepped out of the carriage and were immediately greeted by an elderly woman.

"Shady!" she said loudly. "Thank you so much for repairing my porch handrail. Here's a little something for you."

She handed him a large tin box of Christmas

cookies.

"Not necessary, Mrs. Tortorici, but much appreciated by my belly," Shady responded.

They hadn't taken five steps before another elderly woman shoved a bag into his arms. "This is for all the times you have changed out the lightbulbs in my house that I couldn't reach," she said. Inside the bag were loaves of freshly baked bread and baguettes.

They had just found three seats at a table inside the tent when Mr. Meyers approached. "For all the times you have plowed out my driveway this winter. A 12 pack of my latest ale, and a bottle of McCallan Fine Oak 21. Smooth as silk," Mr. Meyers said with a nod and a wink.

"What the hell?!" Casey exclaimed. "Cookies. Baguettes. Beer. Scotch."

"What can I say? I'm a nice guy."

"I'm nice!"

"Apparently not as nice as I am," Shady smiled. "But don't worry, I'll let you have one of Mrs. Tortorici's peanut butter chocolate drop cookies."

"I don't want your cookies," Casey snipped.

"Ok, Miss Snippy. Then how bout a dance?" He held his hand out for her.

"Fine," she grumbled, as she took it and let him lead her to the dance floor.

It was a slow song so they fumbled around, unsure where to put their arms and how close to stand, but as Taylor Swift sang *Silent Night* in the background, they eventually settled on slowly dancing around the floor, their hands up high and tight with Casey's head resting on Shady's chest. When the song faded to a close, and the bells of the next song began, the people on the dance floor parted and Lindsey appeared. She pointed at Shady and he looked around to make sure she was pointing at him. She nodded yes and then motioned with her pointer finger for him to come to her as Mariah Carey's *All I Want for Christmas* began to play.

"Can you excuse me a minute, Case?"

"Sure," she answered suspiciously as she eyed the woman. "I'm going to get a glass of Prosecco." Turning to Jeremy she asked, "Who is that woman?"

"A teacher at the middle school."

"She's a teacher?"

"I know, right?" Jeremy said.

Shady and Lindsey's dance was a little awkward at first. He wasn't much of a dancer. But she knew how to move. She owned the dance floor and there was some strange symmetry between them. He slid a step or two to one side and then the other. She moved around him and up against him ever so slightly. When Shady did the face wipe with his right hand, the room erupted and he began to laugh.

Then he spun her around, walked her back and pulled her close. He was clearly enjoying himself. It was a side of him people rarely saw.

"I think that's the happiest I've ever seen Shady," one woman remarked.

"I think he looks stupid," Casey grumbled as she sipped her Prosecco.

***

The party had begun to wind down a few hours later--only 50 or so die hards remained-- when Jeremy approached his sister. "Everyone's headed to Smarty's," he said.

"Who's everyone?" she asked.

"Me. Shady. Lindsey. And about 30 other people."

"The whore is going?"

"She's not a whore," Jeremy smiled. "She's a middle school teacher. And she's nice," he added.

"Whatever."

"Ok, Miss Snippy. Well, if you'd like to join us, that's where we'll be."

"I'm not snippy!" Casey protested. "There's just something about her I don't like."

"Hell hath no fury like a woman scorned..." he mumbled under his breath.

"What did you just say?"

"You heard me."

"You don't even know what that's from. You failed 8th grade English."

"I know enough to know that you hate not being the prettiest girl in the room for a change. And you're certainly not the most fun."

"That's not what this is about," she said defensively.

"So are you coming or not, Miss Snippy?"

She looked across the dance floor at Shady holding court with Lindsey and the young fun crowd that still remained. He nodded at Casey and smiled when he noticed her looking.

"Fine," she said. "But I'm not snippy."

"Whatever you say," Jeremy answered.

Smarty's was located in a large building that was formerly an inn and had housed at varying times a Chinese restaurant and a comedy club among other businesses. Located in the heart of Main Street in downtown, it looked over the Niantic Harbor and had long been a staple for locals and tourists alike. One side of the place was a bright, family style restaurant, while the other, a dark Pub with a bar and plenty of televisions for the locals to root on their beloved Patriots, Celtics, Bruins and Red Sox — simply called "the Sox" by the locals. Anyone who rooted for a team other than the ones mentioned above were looked at with extreme suspicion, including Shady, who had unusual loyalties to the Dallas Cowboys and New York Mets. The first because he was raised in Dallas. The second because the Mets were the first pro baseball team he saw play in person and he had always liked underdogs. The locals largely left him alone in spite of these two obvious character flaws because, well, he was bigger and stronger than just about everyone else.

Normally quiet by midnight, the night of the Christmas Ball was always one of Smarty's biggest nights of the year. The Ball had spilled into the bar and it wasn't long before shots of varying degrees of difficulty were lined up along and around the horseshoe bar. A giant catcher's mitt of a hand reached out into the crowd and pulled Casey in.

"Lindsey. This is Casey. Case. Lindsey," he said by way of introduction.

"Ahhhh. Now it makes sense," Lindsey responded with a nod.

"What makes sense?" Casey asked curiously and with a tinge of annoyance.

Jeremy chomped down on a handful of popcorn and grinned as if he was enjoying a movie.

"Nothing," Lindsey shrugged. "Just that you're beautiful."

"Thank you. I think," Casey responded, blushing slightly.

"She's smart as well," Shady interjected. "She's a lawyer."

"Is there really a need for one in a town this small?"

"Are you kidding? There's a state prison three miles down the road. Three quarters of her clients are there."

"That's not true!" Casey laughed as she punched him in the arm. "I do mostly small stuff. Real estate. Wills. Speeding tickets."

"No murder trials?" Lindsey asked.

"No. We haven't had a murder here in twenty years."

"They just send all the murderers here," Shady remarked.

"I understand you're a teacher," Casey said.

"Yes. There might be a murder here before too long. I'd like to kill a few of the little shits," Lindsey responded before adding, "Kids just have no accountability these days."

She was perhaps a bit coarser than Casey was used to, especially for a middle school teacher. But she was interesting and likable enough, although completely wrong for Shady, Casey determined after knowing her for all of two minutes.

Shady began passing whiskey shots all around. "Merry Christmas!" he said, hoisting his shot high into the air.

"Merry Christmas!!!" the chorus of people responded.

VII ~Whearl Campbell~

Jeremy pulled his white Cowboys #22 jersey over his head and went downstairs. His sister looked up from her coffee with a bit of surprise.

"Not exactly Christmas apparel," she said.

"It's better. Emmitt Smith's game jersey," Jeremy answered. "Not that you would know who he is."

"I know who Emmitt Smith is. The guy who won Dancing with the Stars."

"Yeah, he's a little better known for being a Hall of Fame running back who won three Super Bowls and for being the NFL's all-time leading rusher."

"Not to me he's not. And I've never understood why men think that them wearing their team's jersey while watching a game on TV actually helps their team."

"Well, I won't be watching it on TV," Jeremy said quietly.

"I beg your pardon?"

Almost as if on cue, the doorbell rang and Shady appeared wearing Troy Aikman's #8 jersey.

"Mr. Miller gave Shady two tickets to the Cowboys-Patriots game for Christmas as a thank you for him helping him with his back patio."

"And that's wonderful for Shady. He's a grown man and if he'd like to spend Christmas in freezing cold weather at a football game, he's certainly entitled to do that."

"You seem to forget I'm a grown man, too," Jeremy laughed. "I'm 26."

"And it's Christmas."

"It's also Cowboys-Patriots. They only play once every four years. In New England only once every eight. And they haven't both been good in the same year in about 30 years."

"Jeremy. It's Christmas," Casey pleaded in a last ditch effort.

"The game is at noon. We'll be back by 5:00," before adding as an afterthought, "unless it goes into overtime..."

The last part was a bit muffled since he was headed for the door and walking away from her.

"What did you say?"

"Nothing, Case. See you later," he said, pulling the door shut behind Shady and him.

"You waited until today to tell her?" Shady asked as they climbed into his truck.

"Less time for her to lay the guilt trip," was Jeremy's response.

"Good thinking."

"Besides, it's Christmas. You can't get mad at someone on Christmas."

"Never underestimate a woman's ability to get angry," Shady warned.

Gillette Stadium was actually located closer to Providence than Boston, which is why the team changed names from the Boston Patriots to the New England Patriots after moving to Foxboro, Massachusetts in 1971. Boston still called the team its own, as did most of New England, which included Rhode Island, Connecticut, New Hampshire, Vermont and to a lesser extent, Maine.

Jeremy had grown up a Patriots fan because of his father, but when both of his parents passed away, Shady became his father figure/older brother/best friend and Shady was raised just outside of Dallas. It was easy to make the change of allegiance since the Cowboys were "America's Team" and on national TV nearly every week.

Although Gillette Stadium was only an hour and fifteen minutes away, Jeremy had only been there one other time, when Shady had brought him there for his 18th birthday, which happened to be the last time the Cowboys were in town. The Cowboys were terrible that year. The Pats were good and smoked them while a drunk Pats fan dumped a beer on Shady and Jeremy because they were wearing Cowboys jerseys. Shady could have pummeled the guy into oblivion, but chose to instead buy him another beer, which the guy proceeded to dump on them as well, although the second time not on purpose. Jeremy hoped the experience would be better this time.

"We should have just parked in Niantic and walked here. 40 bucks for the privilege of walking two miles to the stadium," Jeremy groaned as they followed throngs of people as if they were all going on some strange pilgrimage.

"It hasn't been that long of a walk. Besides, the further the walk now, the easier it will be getting out later," Shady reasoned.

Everyone loved a winner, that much was clear.

The last time they saw the Cowboys in New England, there were scarcely any Dallas fans in attendance. What a difference a few more wins made. Big, navy blue "D" flags flew high above tailgates. Cowboys jerseys were plentiful in the parking lots. One such tailgate spotted Aikman and Smith walking together and waved them over.

"Nice to see some Cowboy fans in enemy territory," the man said with a slight Texas drawl. "Have a beer, boys."

The man was fifty something, tall, rugged, with sandy brown hair and a neatly trimmed mustache. He was sporting a cowboy hat and a Roger Staubach home jersey.

"Help yourselves to an Italian sausage as well," he offered.

"Thank you. Much appreciated," Shady answered.

"You from Dallas?" the man asked.

"Was born and raised just outside of it."

"Whereabouts?"

"Southlake."

"You go to Carroll?" the man asked, perking up even more now.

"Yes, sir."

"I'm from Allen. When did you go there?"

"Early 90's."

"You were a few years after me, but you played for Ledbetter?"

Shady nodded.

"Man, you guys used to steamroll us."

"Back when we were both mid-sized schools. You guys are top of the heap now."

"Yeah we've had a good run of late. You a lineman back in the day?"

"Fullback."

"There was one tough sunovabitch back then. Big as a house running back. Fast too. Sal somebody. Can't remember his last name. That wasn't you by any chance was it?"

Shady smiled. "State Champs '92 and '93."

"I'll be damned. I had a cousin playing during that time. He used to say tackling you was like trying to tackle a freight train that had come off the tracks. Do you still live in the Big D?"

"No. Moved to Connecticut about 15 years ago. How about you?"

"Went to SMU undergrad and Law School then took a job in New York City. I get back home a couple of times a year and see the Cowboys every time they come in to play the Giants. I'm Bob."

"Shady. And this is Jeremy."

"Shady! That's right. So big that if you stood anywhere near him you were in the shade," the man laughed as he explained the nickname to Jeremy. "You look like you can still play a little."

"Those days are long gone I'm afraid."

"Ever play any college ball?"

"No. Never did. Last game I ever played was the '93 state championship game."

"You must have had offers."

"A few. But college wasn't for me."

"Well, it's nice to meet you. We're heading into the stadium shortly, but if you'd like to stop by after the game, we will be here."

"Thank you, but if we're late for Christmas dinner this young man will be living on my couch and he's a slob," Shady said, pointing at Jeremy.

Jeremy rolled his eyes. "Let's go, Sal."

"If you repeat that to anyone, they won't be able to identify your body with dental records," Shady responded while they walked.

***

Their seats were as advertised. The first row behind the Cowboys bench on the 30 yard line. The game was even better. After the Cowboys led for most of it, Tom Brady marched the Patriots down the field for a touchdown with fourteen seconds left. Up 1, they decided to go for 2, to ensure no worse than overtime, but Brady was hit just as he released the ball and his pass was intercepted in the end zone with nothing but the great green yonder between the Cowboys cornerback and victory. 104 yards later, the Gillette Stadium crowd was stunned into silence, save for a few dozen pockets of Cowboys fans that were wildly celebrating the blown two point conversion.

"I can't believe it! I can't believe it!" Jeremy screamed as he jumped up and down.

But Shady's excitement was tempered as he pointed to the little yellow flag on the field. The play was called back for pass interference and the Pats converted their second chance to take a 3 point lead. The stadium was literally shaking at that point. Until a little known kickoff returner from Idaho State went 77 yards with the kickoff to set up the game tying field goal. Overtime it was.

"We're dead," Jeremy said matter-of-factly.

"We can still win this."

"I'm not talking about the game."

"Right," Shady nodded in agreement. "Well, not much we can do about that. Might as well enjoy ourselves."

The police security patrol that was on the field edged closer to the stands as the game headed to overtime. The one closest to Shady and Jeremy squinted as he grew closer to make certain his eyes weren't playing tricks on him.

"Shady?" he asked.

Shady appeared to recognize the man right away, "Hey, Bill," he answered slightly uncomfortably.

"What are you doing here?" Bill asked while reaching over the wall to give him a hug like a long lost brother.

"I live up this way now."

"No shit? Man, you just up and vanished on us all," Bill said.

"Yeah. Thought it was time to live somewhere new. What are you doing is the big question?"

"Retired from the force. Doing private security now and I travel with the team. Pretty good gig. It's good to see you, man. You look great."

It was at that moment that the same kick returner from Idaho State, took the opening kickoff in overtime and raced the length of the field for the winning score. The Cowboys had won.

"I gotta go," Bill said in a hurry, rushing out onto the field to protect coaches and players, before turning back around to motion for Shady to call him.

***

"How do you know that cop from the game?" Jeremy asked once they were in the car.

"I grew up with him. Went to high school with him. Played football with him..."

"What a day this has been," Jeremy proclaimed. "The Cowboys won and I got a glimpse into the life of Shady Badesso!"

"Not that much of a glimpse," Shady countered.

"I know that you were a football star. How many yards did you rush for in high school?"

"I don't know. A few thousand." Shady downplayed it even though he probably could have told Jeremy to the exact yard.

"And you won two state championships."

"Yes."

"And Texas is big boy football. That's impressive. I also learned how you got your nickname."

"Shady wasn't my only nickname."

"No?"

"They used to call me Whearl Campbell."

"Because of how you whirled around the field?"

"They spelled it W-H-E-A-R-L. As in the white Earl Campbell, because I used to run over people like he did."

It was unusual to hear Shady talk about himself, but it made him feel better to do it. Not talking much about his life pre-Niantic all these years had almost made him feel as though he never had a childhood.

"Whearl Campbell," Jeremy said with a smile. "I like that a lot better than 'Sal'."

"What's wrong with Sal?"

"Sounds like an old Italian guy that works in a butcher shop."

Shady chuckled as they continued up the road.

"This old truck of yours go any faster?" Jeremy asked.

"Sure. Why?"

"Because I just got a text from my sister that Lindsey is already there, so unless you are a fool and want to give them time to exchange secrets about you, I'd drop that pedal to the metal."

Shady hit the gas and the old V-8 let out a scream and begin to whearl up the highway.

***

The two women appeared to be sizing each other up in silence. Casey in jeans wearing a red sweater with green Christmas trees on it.

Lindsey in a form fitting, green dress that was just short enough to cause some confusion as to whether it was a shirt or dress. Casey was sipping a glass of white wine. Lindsey drinking a Corona out of the bottle.

"So when did you move to the area?" Casey asked breaking the awkward silence.

"I came in June. Been here about six months now."

"And how do you like it?"

"I like it well enough. The people are nice. The area is beautiful. Boston is close. New York City isn't too far away. Beach is right down the road."

"What brought you here to begin with?"

"Was just driving through I guess. Seemed like as good of a place as any to stop."

"Are you planning on staying long?"

"Haven't figured that out yet. Maybe. I tend to not stay in any one place that long though."

"Any particular reason for that?" Casey asked in a tone that was more accusatory than questioning.

"Is that a bad thing?" Lindsey resounded. Nothing really rattled her.

"Only if you're looking to settle down I suppose."

"I just never wanted to be one of those people that grew up in a small town, got too comfortable, and never left."

She had just described Casey's life in one sentence. "Is there something wrong with that?" Casey asked, returning the question.

"Not for some people," Lindsey smiled as the door flew open and the boys walked in just in the nick of time.

"What did we miss?" Shady asked with a breathlessness that indicated he had run to the front door.

"Absolutely nothing," Casey answered. "We were just getting to know each other. Beer?"

"Sure," Shady answered skeptically.

"Dinner will be ready in about 15 minutes."

The dining room table was beautifully decorated as was pretty much everything in the house. It was tasteful and classy, without being over the top or overly expensive. The four of them were seated boy/girl around the oval table.

"What a great game today must have been to see," Lindsey said.

"If you were a Cowboys fan, yes," Shady answered.

"We ran into some other Cowboys fans tailgating outside the stadium and it turns out Shady here was some sort of Texas football legend," Jeremy added.

"Oh really?" Lindsey asked, intrigued.

"Yup. Two state titles. Star running back. Whearl Campbell."

"Whearl Campbell?" they all laughed hysterically. All except Shady of course.

"As in the white Earl Campbell. Not that you probably have any idea who that is."

"I know who he is," Casey said defensively. "That old country singer."

"Not Glen Campbell, dingbat," Jeremy said and they all enjoyed a laugh at her expense.

She took it well, smiling and laughing with them with the slightest hint of a reddish tint of embarrassment on her face. Shady had always loved that about her. Her ability to laugh at herself was possibly her most endearing quality in a long list of qualities. They were still laughing when Shady's phone rang. He glanced down at it and saw that it was his mother calling.

"Aren't you going to answer it?" Casey asked. "It's your mother. And it's Christmas."

He nodded and excused himself from the table. "Merry Christmas, mom."

His greeting was followed by a long silence before, "Ok, mom. I'm on my way."

They stared at him in silence having only heard one half of a brief and what appeared to be serious conversation.

"My father died," Shady explained.

VIII ~Home at Last~

Southlake, Texas was a small suburb of Dallas and the 4th wealthiest city in the country, known for a large shopping complex and its high school football team, but it wasn't always known for either. Most people attributed the boom in population and wealth to two things— its proximity to the Dallas/Fort Worth International Airport which opened in 1974, and the decision to maintain only one high school instead of two like many other towns of a similar size. The first was good for business. The second was good for the football team, as the larger pool of students, along with a legendary coach, allowed them to become a state powerhouse.

Born Salvatore Badissimo to an elementary school teacher and a commercial real estate mogul who would later build the Southlake Town Square, one of the most popular shopping centers in the Dallas Metro area, Sal was a popular student and a great athlete, both of which were capable of opening many doors for him. But "Shady" as he would come to be known, never wanted to follow in his father's footsteps, which led to some stress and strain in their relationship for a time, until his father came to accept that Shady was simply a man meant to work with his hands. Cars. Trucks. Buildings. He could do it all with very little instruction. The latter came in handy on many of his father's projects, but Shady wanted more. He wanted to do something with a purpose, but after foregoing many college offers from his high school football days, his options were somewhat limited. He decided on the police academy and he was an instant success. Strong and tough, he also possessed a keen analytical mind with the ability to know how people thought, sometimes before they knew themselves.

He quickly progressed through the academy and soon found himself on the streets of Dallas, on the fast track to becoming a detective. One afternoon changed all that, and he suddenly moved out of state, still speaking to his parents regularly, but only seeing them when they came to visit him in Connecticut. If there was a reason for his falling out with his hometown and chosen profession, residents of Niantic either didn't know about it or didn't care. They had adopted him as one of their own.

***

Shady hadn't seen his mother in nearly four

years and hadn't stepped foot in Dallas in nearly fourteen, when he walked down the exit ramp into the DFW Airport terminal. She looked pretty much the same, albeit with a couple of additional wrinkles and a few strands of grey hair, and he could not help but wonder how his mother viewed him. He had wrapped a few extra pounds around the waistline in recent years, but was still a youngish 42.

"Welcome home," she said with a warm smile as she hugged her only child tightly.

They drove along a white picket fence for what seemed like an eternity, before turning in past the stone pillars. The gate opened to a long, white-washed stone driveway which arched in front of the sprawling Texas ranch-style home with an open air front porch that ran the entire length of the house. Shady's parents had lived there for all 43 years of marriage and it was the only house Shady had ever known. Many a night had been spent on the porch watching the sun set or looking up at the stars while two dogs, always two, romped across the vast yard. Almost as if on cue, a chubby, black Labrador retriever ambled out.

"Only one dog these days?" Shady asked.

The words were still floating in the air when the screen door was nosed open and a tiny yellow lab with soft puppy fur and an angelic face, bounded out. Shady knelt down on the porch to make himself less imposing to the puppy, and the dog leapt into his arms and began showering him with puppy kisses.

His father had always said during times of sadness, *When one life ends, another begins.*

"How did he die, mom?"

"He had a stroke."

"I know. But had he been sick?"

"Not at all. Clean bill of health just a week earlier. He sat down to watch the evening news and went to sleep. He never woke back up. Doctor thinks a piece of plaque broke off his heart valve and caused the stroke."

"I guess if you're going to go, that's the way to go. No pain and suffering. No idea that it's about to happen. Not so great for the people that find you though."

"No, it was not," his mother assured him. "I keep wondering if I should have noticed sooner and if I had, if anything could have been done. He just looked like he was sleeping. Just as he had a million times before."

"That's silly. First of all, he probably died instantly."

"That's what the doctor said."

"Well, there you have it. Besides, what were you supposed to do? Slide a mirror under his nose at all times to make sure he was breathing? He wasn't even sick."

"I know."

"I'm sorry I didn't make it back on time for the wake," Shady said. "I had to tie up a few loose ends before leaving."

"You're here now. That's all the matters. Do you want to speak at the funeral tomorrow?" his mother asked.

"I don't think so. I don't want to be a distraction."

"Why would you be a distraction? You're his son."

"People have long memories."

"When are you going to forgive yourself for what happened?"

When Shady didn't answer, she knew the answer was *never*.

"Your friends all miss you. Lisa DeShay's sister stopped by the wake. I don't know if you've heard, but Lisa is very sick."

"I don't really keep in touch with anyone. What's wrong with her?"

"Inoperable brain tumor. Only has a few months to live. It's awful. Husband and two kids."

"Jesus."

"Her sister said that Lisa made her promise to come by to represent her. Wanted to come herself, but the doctors wouldn't allow it."

"She's always had a big heart. That's so awful. I wish I could do something."

"Why don't you go see her?" his mother suggested. "I'm sure she would appreciate that. You two used to be thick as thieves."

"That was a long time ago."

"She always liked you."

Shady sat silently in a moment of thought before looking back up at his mother. "Where does she live?"

"In the same house she grew up in. Parents bought a smaller home not far away."

"Can I borrow a car?" he asked.

***

He made the drive from memory, the same drive he had made dozens of times as a teenager. Lisa was a couple of years younger than him, but had always been infinitely more mature. She was the anti-cheerleader. Sarcastic and funny, she was a straight shooter. If you didn't want an honest answer, you didn't ask her a question. The area directly around Lisa DeShay was strictly a no bullshit zone. And yet, she was also an extremely kind and caring person who managed to find the good in everyone, no matter how difficult it was to find in some people. She was tough without being judgmental and people appreciated that about her.

The shutters were a different color and the lawn not quite as immaculately cared for as he remembered, but everything else about Lisa

DeShay's house was pretty much the same. He heard a bit of shuffling after ringing the doorbell, before a man opened it with a smile. Tall and thin, the man was cleanly shaven both on his head and face.

"Hi, Shady!" Jim DeShay said with an extended arm looking for a handshake.

Shady shook it and asked, "Have we met before?"

"No, but Lisa gave me an accurate description of you."

"How did she describe me?" Shady asked curiously.

"Like a walking refrigerator."

"How is she?" Shady laughed.

"Not great today. She's been lying down."

"Well, don't bother her then. But please let her know I stopped by."

"Her exact words to me before she went to lay down were, and I quote, 'For the next few hours, don't disturb me unless Shady comes by.'"

She was already out of her bed and into her wheelchair by the time they entered the room.

"I was going to try and do something with my hair today, but I figured I'll be dead in a few weeks anyway, so what's the point? You don't think less of me do you, Shady?" Lisa said with her old familiar energy.

"Of course not," Shady answered with a smile.

Most people in a similar situation to Lisa would push people away, not wanting to be seen and remembered at less than their best, but one of Lisa's most redeeming qualities was a complete lack of vanity and her self-deprecating sense of humor.

"Wheel me out to the patio, will you? Let's get some fresh air."

He pushed her out through the French double doors while her adoring husband looked on, happy to see a smile on her face, no matter how briefly.

"How'd you know I'd come?" Shady asked.

"What kind of a person doesn't visit their dying friend when they're in town?"

"I've been here less than five minutes and you've already talked about dying twice."

"That's because I'm at peace with it, my dear. Well, not really at peace. I'm going to miss Jim and my girls something fierce, but I'm accepting of the idea that someone with a much higher authority than me has something more important in mind for me."

"Only the good die young. Billy Joel sang about it, so it has to be true."

"Enough of this talk about me!" she said, shifting gears to a more serious tone. "I'm so sorry about your dad. He was a really nice man. Were you two still close?"

Shady nodded. "We spoke most days, but I hadn't seen him or my mother in a while."

"How come?"

"I don't get back here very often. Didn't want to saddle them with the attention that comes with it."

"How long are you going to continue to beat yourself up over that? You do realize that in high school, I didn't like you because you were a star athlete. I liked you because you were a star athlete that didn't act like one. Younger players were never hazed because the other players knew you wouldn't allow it. In fact, I remember one night some football players from Westlake showed up at a party and they were giving a wedgie to one of their own players in front of his girlfriend and friends. You calmly walked over and put your hand on one of the players shoulders and shook your head. And they stopped."

"You were there that night?"

"I was always around. Look, darlin, some people judge others on the worst thing they've ever done. Others judge them based on the sum of their deeds. I, on the other hand, believe we are all the best of what we can be, because that's what shows our true potential. And no matter what method we use to judge your life, you my friend, are a good person. You are a kind and gentle soul."

"Thank you, although I'm not sure I agree."

"Promise me something."

"Sure."

"You lost some valuable time with your father. Don't let the same thing happen with your mother because you have a harsh opinion of yourself. Besides, you have to come back here to visit me once I'm gone."

"How can I visit you if you're gone?"

"In the cemetery, dummy. I won't exactly be able to travel to you."

Shady smiled. *When one life ends, another begins.*

***

Jeremy stared at the computer screen in disbelief. He had typed into a Google search "Sal Badesso" but nothing appeared. He then typed "Shady Badesso Carroll High School" and dozens of results appeared.

Badissimo Runs Carroll Past Allen to State Championship

ARLINGTON: Sal "Shady" Badissimo scored three touchdowns and rushed for 220 yards as he ran over, around and through the Allen Eagles....

He typed "Sal Badissimo". Within seconds, hundreds of search items appeared.

Dallas Cop Charged With Police Brutality

Cop Found Not Guilty, Riots Ensue

Police Beating Victim in a Coma

Jeremy would go on to read each and every article on his best friend that he apparently knew nothing about.

IX   *~Anthony Badissimo~*

Anthony Badissimo was born to immigrant parents who arrived through Ellis Island in the early 1900's. His father was a handyman by trade. Carpentry. Cars. Stone work. He could do it all, and worked hard to provide for his family. His mother, however, was the backbone of the family. She was a stay at home mom who loved what she did, and loved their life, but like any mother, wanted more for her children. She pushed Anthony to study hard in hope that it would open doors for him down the road. Both parents preached work ethic, which is why Anthony went to school during the day and worked at an ice cream parlor at night, with football practice sandwiched in between.

Ironically, it was the one thing that came easiest to him, football, that provided the greatest opportunity in the form of a scholarship to Southern Methodist University in Dallas. He had never been to Texas before he enrolled there and he wasn't Methodist. Certainly not a southern Methodist.

After graduating with a degree in business management, he began to work for a small commercial real estate company managing a couple of apartment complexes. He eventually purchased his first building at age 27, using money he had saved up combined with a hefty bank loan. He reimagined the building as an office building and took out a line of credit to make that dream a reality. Not long thereafter he filled the entire building with thriving businesses. Mini-malls were next to conquer, closely followed by the Southlake Town Square, a 127 store upscale shopping mall with restaurants, a Town Hall, municipal court, medical offices, a theatre and a hotel. He was the driving force behind the large management company behind the project, and it ensured that neither he nor generations of his family, would ever need to work again if they didn't want to. And yet you'd never know it from meeting him. He drove an eight year old Ford F-150 pickup truck. He dressed neatly, but not in designer brands and he hadn't seen a suit since his wedding day. In fact, his down to earth nature and complete lack of showiness is what first attracted his wife to him. Forty years later, they still lived in the same house on the same land, as the day they were married. Shady came a year later. His father had bought the home Shady grew up in just as the airport opened and before the real estate market began to soar. The house and land would eventually be worth ten times what it was purchased for.

But Anthony never let his success change who he was. His son was treated well, but not spoiled. He worked while in high school as his father had. And they had dinner together as a family every night, even if it meant waiting until after a game for them to do so. He was a loving husband, a loyal friend, supportive father, and the neighbor all the other kids referred to as Uncle Tone. He played in the Thanksgiving Day football games with the kids, manned the grill at the neighborhood cookouts, and played the bugle at every party. He sang with his friends. He danced with his wife. Not every night, but on special occasions and even the odd weekday morning breakfast.   He laughed with his family and friends and cried whenever any of them were suffering. And so it was. A great life with a great family, cut way too short. And the rest were left to carry on without him.

***

Shady strode to the lectern in the church wearing enough material on his 48 Regular suit to make a tent to cover two hundred people. Clean shaven, his hair gently gelled, with broad shoulders that made his back look like it could have fit a drive-in movie screen on it, Shady looked like a Clark Kent-type super hero.

"My father," he began, "had a terrible singing voice, but it never stopped him from torturing others with it. His nickname in the neighborhood was 'Uncle Tone'. He thought it was because his name was Tony, but in reality, it was because he was tone deaf.

He didn't know how to play the bugle, but that didn't stop him from trying. He brought his bugle to every party he attended and played Reveille at the beginning and Taps at the conclusion, although he was so awful that it was sometimes difficult to tell the difference between the two.

He was the worst driver you've ever heard about. One friend called the experience of leaving the Texas Stadium parking lot with my dad behind the wheel one of the most harrowing experiences of his life, and the man fought in two wars. I'm also not sure what that says about me, since he's the one who taught me to drive.

He wasn't the grill master he considered himself to be either. His idea of seasoning was salt and his idea of marinating was pepper, but if you enjoyed your burger with the shape, size and consistency of an NHL hockey puck, then he was your man.

He couldn't find the dishwasher with a road map, and couldn't operate the washing machine or dryer if you left him instructions and gave him five tries. But we all forgave him for his shortcomings, because he had so many strengths and because we loved him.

We loved him because he was a family man. He brought my mother fresh flowers every week because he wanted her to have something to look at that was nearly as beautiful as she was without having to look in the mirror.

He was supportive as a father. I don't recall him ever missing one of my football games, and he was never critical of how I played. He'd manage to find the one good thing I'd done. 'Man, you really pancaked that linebacker in the 4th quarter,' he'd say. After I responded with how horrible I'd been the rest of the game, he'd simply say, 'If you were perfect, life would be boring. Now let's go get a pizza.'

He was a loyal friend who had many of the same close friends the day he died as he did in 1st grade and it didn't matter how many miles separated them.

He was kind. Looking out at this room today, I'm going to guess that there are probably a hundred people in here that spent at least one holiday at our house, because my father wanted to make sure no one ever spent a holiday alone.

And he was funny. Yes, he told some of the corniest jokes imaginable, but his laughter was so contagious, you couldn't help but laugh as well. I know today of all days, he would be pissed if he saw anyone crying. He would much rather see people laughing at his idiosyncrasies, and smiling at the memories you all created with him. If this was a bar, I'd ask you to raise your glasses in a toast, but since it's a church, I ask that you simply hug the person next to you in a celebration of the life of Anthony 'Uncle Tone' Badissimo."

***

"You were simply magnificent, my dear," Lisa told Shady when he stopped by on his way out of town.

"You were there?"

"My sister recorded it. Smart. Funny. Sweet. I want you to give the eulogy at my funeral," she said matter-of-factly.

"I'm fairly certain that you could find someone to do it who you've seen a bit more frequently in the past fifteen years."

"You knew me when I was young, healthy and fun. I don't want someone blabbering on about how great I was and making everyone cry. I want people to laugh. Tell me a joke, Shady."

"Now, you're putting me on the spot."

"Please?" she begged.

"Ok," he said after a moment's hesitation. "A lady goes into her doctor's office for a checkup and the nurse pulls out a needle and vial to take her blood. 'You're going to feel a little prick,' the nurse says. 'I doubt it,' the lady answers, 'I've had two kids.'"

There was the slightest pause and then Lisa burst out laughing. The loudest laugh she had enjoyed in months, to the point where she started coughing and her husband ran into the room to make sure she was all right.

"I'm fine," she waved. "Shady told a joke."

"Must have been a good one," her husband chuckled.

"Not really. But an A for effort." Turning to Shady she said, "You are definitely speaking at my funeral. Promise me."

"If you insist."

"I do. And no tears. Just laughter."

"I may need to go for a little slapstick and trip going up the stairs of the church."

"Just don't drop the casket," she warned.

"So now I'm a pallbearer as well?? I've got to give the eulogy and be a pallbearer. Anything else? What are *you* going to do?"

"I've got the hardest job, my dear. I've got to die."

"That doesn't sound so tough," Shady responded without missing a beat. "You've just got to lie there and hold your breath."

She laughed out loud again. "You're awful!"

"A little irreverence never hurt anyone."

"Irreverent! That's what I want my eulogy to be."

"You want me to roast you at your funeral?" Shady said skeptically. "I'm not sure your husband and kids would appreciate that."

"Oh, but they would. Include them in it. They could tell you stories."

"I'm sure they could."

"So it's settled."

"I'm not so sure how comfortable I am with this."

"I want people to laugh. I want people to cringe. And I want people to gasp and look around because they aren't sure whether they should laugh or cringe. Every funeral I've been to people say the same dumb things. You'd think we had 400 million Mother Teresa's in the world. I'm not perfect. I know it. I'm a smart ass. I've forgotten one of my kid's birthdays before. I've yelled at my husband for not rinsing his dirty dish out and leaving it in the sink."

"I don't think any of those things are that horrible. Well, maybe forgetting your kid's birthday."

"Yes. I'm a horrible person," she laughed.

"You're hardly a horrible person."

"I fooled around with Derek Summers back in high school," she blurted out.

"Wasn't he dating Janie?"

"Yup."

"And wasn't Janie your best friend?"

"Yuuuup. But I had six wine coolers and made the hell out with him," she exclaimed proudly.

"You really are a horrible person," Shady laughed.

"Eh, I did her a favor. He ended up flunking out of college, robbed a liquor store and ended up in jail. I think he identifies himself as a woman now."

"I'm sure Janie is forever grateful."

"She should be. She married the grandson of the SoftPillow fortune."

"Does she know you fooled around with her high school boyfriend?"

"Oh lord no. Maybe leave that out of the eulogy."

"You can't pick and choose what goes in a roast."

"I can do whatever I like. It's my funeral."

"You won't be there."

"You are truly awful. What kind of a person would say nasty things about someone when they aren't there to defend themselves?"

"You said you wanted me to roast you!" Shady exclaimed.

"I'm joking," she laughed. "Roast away. But feel free to use your judgment as to what might make someone else hate me for all of eternity."

"I'll do my best."

She glanced at the clock on the wall. "You better hurry or you're going to miss your flight."

"It has truly been a pleasure," Shady said. "I'm sorry it's been so long."

"Yes, it has. And don't worry about it. You've just made my life complete. Don't be offended if the next time you see me, I'm not very talkative because I'm dead."

"Good lord, woman. Have you no filter?"

"My filter broke the day I learned to talk and they were never able to fix it. I love you, Shady boy," Lisa said as she reached up to hug her friend.

"I love you, too," he answered, wiping a single tear from his cheek before she could notice.

X ~*Prison Break*~

*T*he text message came through just after his plane touched down in Providence.

Can I give you a rain check for our slumber party? I have an early morning and long day at school tomorrow. Glad you're back. I've missed you!

Truth be told, Shady wasn't that disappointed to receive the text. He was exhausted mentally and physically and wanted nothing more than to dive face first, spread eagle onto his bed and sleep until dawn.

As he drove along the coast back to Niantic from Rhode Island, Shady's mind wandered. Being home for the first time in years had created such conflicting emotions for him. It wasn't unlike when you saw an old friend for the first time in years. When you left them again, you began to miss them immediately, but you also began to wonder if you saw them all the time, if things would remain the same. Could you really go home again?

Was Niantic home now because he had been there so long? Because they had accepted him as one of their own? Or because he didn't have any other choice? Maybe it was a combination of all three.

He pulled into his driveway and felt the instant pangs of loneliness that came with being single at 42. He unpacked his clothes and hung up his suit that he hoped he wouldn't need to wear again for quite some time. Just as he pulled back the covers on his bed, his phone buzzed again and another message appeared.

Are you back?

This time he called the number instead of texting.

"Hey there," Casey answered. "How'd it go? I mean, I'm sure it didn't go well, but, you know what I mean..."

"It actually went better than expected. I got to see my mom, say goodbye to my dad, and spend some time with an old friend who is dying of cancer."

"Jesus. That's better than expected?"

"Well, yeah. Obviously, I wish I could have said goodbye to my dad while he was still alive..."

"There's nothing you could have done about that. He wasn't even sick."

"I know, but I feel badly I didn't spend that much time with him in recent years," Shady explained.

"I'm sure he understood that. Where did your dad grow up?"

"Queens."

"And your grandparents stayed there?"

"Til the day they died."

"But your dad moved to Dallas."

"It's where he went to college."

"And I'm sure his parents understood."

"Sure. Because he was making a life for himself. I work in a hardware store."

"You are much more important to this town than you'll ever realize," Casey scolded.

"Why? Because I fix a few handrails and plow some driveways? Those people could get any high school kid to do those things for ten bucks an hour."

"Because you do them for free. And without people even having to ask. You set the standard of goodness, Shady. Whether you realize it or not."

"Can't say as I agree," Shady disagreed, "but thanks."

"Now tell me about your friend. That sounds awful."

"Lisa is a couple of years younger than me, but we were great friends in high school. She was the voice of reason that always kept me level headed. She was smart and funny and didn't give a rats patootie what anyone said about her. We lost touch over the years, but when my mom told me she was sick, I decided to go visit her."

"And how is she?"

"She's not feeling well, you can tell, but she refuses to give in to it. It's almost as if she doesn't want to let Cancer see that it's getting the better of her."

"She sounds tough."

"Tough as nails. Always has been. It's funny. Some people, no matter how much time has passed, when you see them again, it's as if you had seen them the day before. But I feel terrible for her. Great husband and two adorable kids."

"There's nothing they can do?" Casey asked.

"It doesn't sound like it. Sounds like it's a matter of time, and all she and her family can do is prepare for the inevitable."

"I'm really sorry."

"Me too, Case. Me too," Shady lamented. "So what's new with you?"

"Oh, you know me. Nothing is ever new. Just closed on a restaurant for a client."

"Whereabouts?"

"Down by the harbor. Good thing about my practice is that I get a lot of repeat customers since most restaurants go out of business within five years. It's kind of like being a doctor that delivers babies and owns a funeral home."

Shady let out a hearty chuckle. "I'm starting to fall asleep, Case. Not because of your conversation," he quickly corrected. "Just been a long week."

"I won't take offense. Dinner soon?"

"Absolutely. Goodnight."

He rolled over and plugged his phone into the charger before turning off the light in his bedroom. He was asleep within minutes.

***

The day began like most every day for Shady with his alarm going off at 7:00am. He sipped a cup of coffee and washed down a couple pieces of white toast with a glass of orange juice while watching the morning edition of SportsCenter. He was on the road toward Clough's by 8:00, rapping the steering wheel to the beat of the music. He thought he heard a siren going off in the distance, but his truck engine was loud which forced him to turn up the music inside it even louder. He found Jeremy and Old Man Clough huddled around the TV inside the store when he entered.

"Did you hear the siren?" Jeremy asked.

"I thought I heard something, but I had my music on pretty loud," Shady replied. "What happened? A fire?"

"Prison break," Jeremy announced while Old Man Clough nodded affirmatively.

"No shit?"

"Two old boys with rap sheets like Dillinger," Earl said.

"John *'Bates'* Carideo and Steven *'Bones'* Smith," Jeremy declared. "Bates as in Norman from Psycho because he slashed up two people and Bones because he helped bury the bodies."

Shady didn't respond. He was fixated on the television.

"Shortly after 8:00am this morning, guards at the Niantic Annex, a Maximum Security State prison, discovered two prisoners were not in their cells. John Carideo and Steve Smith are believed to have escaped through the laundry room, but authorities do not know how they escaped off the grounds," the reporter announced. "Tracking dogs followed a path through the woods to this house..."

"That's Lindsey's house," Shady said as he bolted for the door.

Jeremy ran after him while yelling back to Old Man Clough, "Be back in a bit, Earl!"

"I've got it covered," Earl waved.

Shady already had his truck started and had begun to pull away when Jeremy pounded on the passenger window for him to open the door. He reached across and pulled the knob up. Jeremy hopped in.

Lindsey's road was a hub of police activity. Her driveway was closed off with police tape while a local officer stood guard. Of course Shady knew him. It was a small town.

"Hey, Shady, what are you doing out here?" the cop asked.

"The girl who lives in this house. Is she..."

"I don't really know anything to be honest. The Stateys and Feds have taken over. Whose place is it?"

"Lindsey Thompson. Teaches at the middle school."

"How do you know her?"

"I'm sort of dating her. Can you let me through, Jeff? I might be able to help them."

Jeff thought it over for a moment before nodding and pulling back one of the cones. A State Trooper greeted Shady at the top of the driveway.

"How'd you get up here?" the Statey growled.

"The woman who lives here is my girlfriend."

"Is your girlfriend Harold McFadden? Because that's who lives here."

"He owns the house. She rents from him. Is she here?"

"I really can't share any information right now."

"I need to know that she's ok," Shady repeated.

"She's not here. No one is," Statey answered at last.

"I might be able to help if you let me look around," Shady offered.

"Afraid not."

"From what I can see, you need all the help you can get."

"Is that so?"

"They're not on foot for starters."

"Well, if they steal a car, we'll know about it."

"They already stole one. Her car is gone."

"What does she drive?"

"A Navy blue, Jeep Patriot.   2012. Connecticut plates."

The Statey finally relented and motioned for Shady to join him in the house. When Jeremy tried to follow them, he was denied entry, and nodded acceptingly. They returned outside a few minutes later.

"See anything unusual?" Jeremy asked.

"Not really," Shady answered.

A crackle in the woods behind the house caused widespread panic. Three officers drew their guns.

"Is that a bear?" one of them asked, when a large, black head appeared on the ridge.

"It's a dog," Shady responded, gently nudging the officer's gun downward. "Big Show!" he yelled.

The giant black lab's ears perked up and he came charging toward Shady, leaping into his arms when he was a few feet away, nearly bowling him over.

"Hey, pal. Where's your mom? Were you on a walkabout when they came?"

"That her dog?" Statey asked.

"Yup. He wanders off sometimes. Probably was gone when they showed up. I'll take him for now."

Shady opened the door to his truck and The Big Show jumped in. He plopped himself directly in the middle of Shady and Jeremy, sitting straight up like a human.

"Now what?" Jeremy asked.

"Big Show is a tracking dog. He'll lead us to her."

"How's he going to do that?"

"By scent," Shady responded as he pulled one of Lindsey's shirts out from underneath his jacket.

"You took it from the crime scene?"

Shady nodded.

"You already said she's not on foot."

"Doesn't matter. His nose is strong and this is one of her favorite shirts. "He'll lead us to her."

XI ~Bates & Bones~

Most studies showed that violent criminals came from lower socioeconomic backgrounds, and had tainted family lives of abuse or a general lack of interest on the part of their parents, but that wasn't the case for Steve Smith. He grew up in a small, farming community in rural Connecticut to middle class parents. His parents both worked, his father as the business manager at the high school and his mother at a florist shop in town, but both were always home for dinner with the family every night. They were supportive of any activity he and his brother participated in, whether it be doing the lighting for the school play, Math League, or the junior varsity swim team.

Elementary school was relatively uneventful, as kids at that age were generally less judgmental and mean spirited than older kids could be. Middle school marked a change as parents had enough time to influence the beliefs of their children, and kids had begun to form cliques based on certain talents or abilities. And that was Steve's problem. His talents—

lighting, cameras, and computers—weren't widely recognized as important and certainly didn't help make him popular. He withdrew into a world of video games and solitude. His parents did what they could to draw him out, bringing him to events with friends who had kids. The kids would all get along well at that event, but then once back at school the following week, things would go back to the way they were. Kids weren't mean to him. They just weren't overwhelmingly accepting of him, and in return, or maybe on account of that, he found their behavior to be immature. He gravitated towards the teachers for companionship and that was a surefire way of cementing unpopularity in middle school.

High school was a bit different for him on two fronts. The first was that his talents became a bit more appreciated. All schoolwork was now done on computers, and he was a wiz with them. Word. PowerPoint. IMovie. A few clicks of a mouse or pad and he could solve your problem. The high school theatre department was also well respected and they were always in need of people to build the staging and set up the lighting. Steve ran the technical aspects of each production from lighting to sound and while that certainly wouldn't confuse him with the quarterback of the football team in terms of popularity, the plays were actually more successful.

The second thing that happened in high school was he befriended a slightly off center, somewhat violent, but strangely amusing character named John Carideo. He was well known, which is to say he wasn't exactly popular, but everyone knew him, mainly because they were afraid of him. If someone from the school were to end up in a bell tower someday with a rifle, he would be everyone's first guess as to who it was. Ironically, he was more bluster than anything back then, but he liked making people feel uneasy around him. It made him feel powerful.

Steve and John met for the first time in Film class. Steve took the class because he thought it would be interesting and he was good at that sort of thing. John took it because it was the path of least resistance. No papers. No exams. Just projects he could pass off onto his other group members.

"You want to partner up for this project?" were the first words he ever spoke to Steve.

Steve nodded and shrugged in acceptance. The project was to make a music video with a public service message within it. John's contribution to the project was to come up with the music. Steve was a little skeptical when the song John chose was Public Enemy's *Harder Than You Think*, but the juxtaposition of Chuck D's hard driving, deep and penetrating lyrics, over views of people doing good deeds for complete strangers made for a powerful video. They both received A's on the project, the first and only A's of their high school career. After that they focused on pranks such as laying a dead fish on the hood of a nemesis teacher's old MG automobile, and tying all of the furniture from the cafeteria to the bottom of the pool. That one earned high praise from their fellow students, but a two week suspension from the school.

By the time they were seniors, it didn't matter what they did or didn't do in class. The teachers just wanted them out, so they passed them along. They were kindred spirits in crime, most of it harmless. They lost touch after graduation, when John entered the Marines, stationed in Camp Lejeune down in the deep south. Steve found himself alone again and floated between relatives in the Midwest working as a mechanic.

They were reunited when both landed in Connecticut eight years later after John finished his tour and Steve moved back home. There was something different about John at this point however, his devilish charm having been replaced by a more hardened darkness. Steve was perhaps the only one who didn't notice. Loneliness will do that to a person. It helped a person look past someone's faults.

It wasn't long before John was fencing diamonds for some unsavory people and when one of those deals went south, he defended himself the way he was trained, by grabbing a handy steak knife, a *very* handy steak knife, and stabbing it through two men's chests, killing them instantly. He then called the only person he knew would help him dispose of the bodies. Steve suggested they break into a local funeral home and cremate them. It wasn't a horrible plan, except the owner lived upstairs and when he awoke to go to the bathroom in the middle of the night, he heard the kiln running downstairs. He stopped it just in time for authorities to identify the bodies.

Chased by both authorities and the mob, they made the calculated move to turn themselves in, figuring they were safer in jail than on the streets. That was true—for a while. But the mob had long reaching arms and sensing it was a matter of time before they reached into the Niantic Annex Federal Prison, John "Bates" Carideo and Steve "Bones" Smith plotted their escape. It took exactly three guards on the payroll to make the move. One to say they were in their cell at night check. One to leave the door to the laundry room open along with leaving some well-placed wire cutters in the corner. And one in the tower to look the other way while they cut a small hole in the wire fence and broke for the woods.

Where they went from there was anyone's guess. Mexico was 1,500 miles to the south.

Canada 400 miles to the north. With an 8 hour head start, either was possible.

XII ~*The Road to Nantucket*~

Shady grabbed a handful of shirts from a drawer and threw them in a duffle bag with a couple pairs of jeans and a pair of backup boots. A toothbrush, some deodorant, and an electric razor in case things got a bit unruly on his face also were making the trip.

Jeremy walked in unannounced just as Shady zipped the duffle closed.

"Where are you going?"

"After Lindsey."

"You have no idea where she is. She could be in Juarez or Saskatchewan for all you know. Why don't you leave it to the authorities?" Jeremy asked.

"Because they don't have a clue what they're doing."

"And you do?"

"More than you think. Besides, I can't just sit here and do nothing."

"Fine. Then I'm coming with you."

"The hell you are."

"The hell I'm not. I'm not letting my best friend go off hunting mass murderers by himself, even if I don't think you've got a fart's chance in a windstorm of finding them."

Shady briefly contemplated taking him versus leaving him behind.

"Your sister would kill me if I let you come," he said at last.

"My sister has no say in the matter. Contrary to what you and her seem to think, I'm a grown man. I'm 26 years old for heaven's sake. And I think she'd be a lot more disappointed that I let my friend head into something potentially dangerous alone."

Shady shook his head before begrudgingly motioning for him to follow him. Jeremy grabbed a backpack from the passenger seat of his car.

"You already packed?"

"If you didn't let me come with you, I was just going to follow you anyway," Jeremy nodded.

Shady motioned for Jeremy to wait before getting into the truck. He let loose a loud whistle and around the corner bounded The Big Show.

"We're bringing the dog? Seriously?" Jeremy asked.

"As I said, he's a tracking dog. He'll come in handy."

Big Show let out a deep *whoof* as if to demonstrate his purpose on the journey.

"Get in, boy," Shady commanded.

The Big Show jumped in and sat like a human on his hind quarters in the middle of the cab. He took up a fair amount of room and sitting straight up, he was actually breathing down on Jeremy.

"Damn, Big Show. You need a breath mint. You could melt steel with that breath," Jeremy cringed.

The dog bowed his head offended.

"You hurt his feelings," Shady said as he patted the dog on the top of his head. It seemed to soften the blow of the insult. His tail was wagging again.

"Where to?" Jeremy asked once they were all situated. "North, South, East or West?"

"That depends," Shady answered as he dialed a number on his cell. After a slight pause, "Jeff. It's Shady. They find that Jeep Patriot yet?"

"Yup. At a park and ride in Baltimore," Jeff answered.

"Anyone report a stolen car in that area?"

"Umm. It's Baltimore," he responded as if that answer should have been obvious.

"So that would be a yes," Shady nodded. "Text me the location of the lot will you?"

"I could get my ass in a sling if they find out, but screw it. The feds were dbags to the locals. Seem to forget one of ours is missing and that we are all on the same team."

"Thanks, bud. I'll let you know if I find anything." He turned to Jeremy. "We're headed to Baltimore."

"So they're headed to Mexico?"

"That remains to be seen."

"Has to be Mexico. Otherwise, why go south to go north? You'd lose your head start."

"They had about an 8 hour head start. True, that's not enough time to go from Niantic to Baltimore and then up to the Canadian Border. But it's also not enough time to get to Mexico."

"Then why not head straight for Canada? They could have gotten across in the middle of the night before they were even reported missing."

"They could have done that. But they'd need some help with passports. They'd have to have someone helping them. Plus, there'd be a record of them crossing. They'd get caught eventually."

"Well, from what I read, they had someone helping on the inside in order to escape. What I don't get is why take a hostage? Insurance I get. Won't be able to shoot them off the road with her in the car. But it has to slow them down and it's only going to make it worse if they get caught. Not to mention, if they do get over the border, what do they do with her then? If they turn her loose, she'll be able to tell people the general area they crossed."

"Now you're thinking like a cop."

"You don't think they'd kill her do you?" Jeremy asked, alarmed now.

"Anything is possible. Which is why I'm not going to wait around for the feds to find her."

Shady pushed down on the gas pedal and his old truck let out a bit of a groan but eventually responded.

***

Five hours, 75 songs on the radio, and a slight delay at the George Washington Bridge later, and they were in Baltimore. Jeremy had been asleep for the last three hours, his head resting on a balled up jacket against the window. Big Show was asleep with his head resting on Jeremy's shoulder. Man's best friend indeed.

The park and ride lot was virtually empty. Some police tape littered the ground around the spot where Lindsey's car must have been.

"So they lose the car here because everyone is looking for it and steal a car. Since it's Baltimore, by the time they figure out which car they took, they've bought themselves even more time. Smart," Jeremy acknowledged.

"You're still thinking like a cop. Now think like a criminal. What buys you even more time?"

"If you get a car that no one will report missing."

"Bullseye."

"Borrowed from someone they know?"

"Possibly," Shady answered only half listening. He was fixated on the somewhat fresh oil spot in the space next to the one where Lindsey's car had been parked.

"What is it?"

"Oil."

"I can see that, Sherlock. But why are you staring at it?"

"The pattern of it. It's a pattern formed by the shape of a hole in the oil pan. Same shape as the one made by the old pickup truck owned by Lindsey's landlord that I helped her get running."

"You think they drove both cars down here and left hers?"

"The way I see it, there are four choices. 1) They are headed to Mexico and driving a stolen car. 2) They drove down here to throw people off and are now headed north to Canada. 3) They drove both cars down and switched right here. Could be headed south or north."

"What's the 4th choice?"

"They're headed somewhere different altogether to hide out until it's easier to cross," Shady answered. "Whichever way they're headed, I'm going to bet it's in that truck. I doubt the feds even know anything about it. I didn't remember it myself until just now."

"You going to call it in so they can track it?"

"I'm going to let Big Show *show* us the way first. Then maybe I'll call it in."

"Why wouldn't you call in? The feds have more access and will be able to track it faster."

"Because they're not going to listen. Because if they swarm the highways, they'll go into hiding. And because some things you just need to do yourself."

Shady pulled Lindsey's shirt from the truck and rubbed it in the Big Show's face.

"Where is she, boy? Which way did she go?"

The dog went wild at the smell of her shirt. He could choose from four directions. With his nose to the ground, he began moving one way. Then another. Then another still. Finally, he settled on North and began sprinting down the road, looking back to make sure they were following him. Shady jumped in the truck and followed the Big Show and Jeremy down the isolated road. He threw open the door when he pulled up alongside of them. Big Show jumped right in, followed by Jeremy.

"This road heads back to the highway heading North."

"Canada it is, eh?" Jeremy stated.

"They'd never make it over."

"You think the dog is wrong?"

"Nope," Shady answered as Big Show slobbered his face in a show of appreciation for his faith in him.

"Where are they then?"

"Somewhere they can hide out until things cool down enough to cross. Somewhere they can cross unnoticed."

"Where then??"

Shady pulled out his phone and googled a map of the northeast on it. He zoomed in at the New England area and pointed to a small spot of land in the Atlantic Ocean just off the coast of Massachusetts.

"Here," he said assuredly.

"Nantucket?"

XIII   ~Two Secrets Revealed~

Shady and Jeremy retraced their path all the way past Niantic before ending up in Cape Cod a little before midnight. Hyannis in January was a veritable ghost town to the point where if someone died or was murdered, the body might not be discovered for weeks.

Along that line of thinking, the Hyannispoint Harbor Inn had been family owned and operated for nearly fifty years, and some of its rooms had started to look like it. But it's close proximity to the Steamship Authority allowed them to charge exorbitant rates from June through September, high enough that they could shut down during the winter months altogether. Even though they didn't need to, the owners kept a portion of the hotel and the bar open on a skeleton crew for the stray guest that happened to need a place for a drink and to lay their head — the bar for the former and a room for the latter.

"What type of room would you like?" the girl behind the counter asked with a somewhat monotone voice. She looked about 25, with

Juicy Couture bottoms and a pink sweatshirt that matched the pink stripe in her ponytail that the kids referred to as an "ombre".

"One with beds in it," Jeremy answered.

"They all have beds. Would you like to be in the old building or new?"

"Whichever is cheaper."

"Old building," she answered without skipping a beat. "King or two twin beds?"

"I'm here with my boy, not my girl."

"So?"

Jeremy shook his head. "Two twins."

"The old rooms don't have enough space for two twin beds."

"Then maybe you should have started out with that question first."

"Two twins. New building. Got it."

"Is there anywhere to get food at this time of night?"

"The bar has food."

"Any good?"

"No, it's terrible," she deadpanned.

Shady was quite enjoying the banter between the two. He figured it unbeknownst to them to be foreplay between the two of them.

"You don't want to share a bed with me?" Shady asked.

"You're so big, the bed doesn't want to share a bed with you."

***

The outdoor bar was zip sealed with plastic windows and doors, and there were only five people inside including Shady and Jeremy. A bartender. A waitress. And the young lady from the front desk.

The waitress was a pleasant woman in her 40's whose wedding band matched that of the bartender, other than hers having a few diamonds on it. They had each arrived in Hyannis separately 20 years ago, both with the intent of staying for a year or two until they figured out what they wanted to do with their lives. They met while working at the hotel, and as so often happened in life, their plans changed. They loved Hyannis during the summer and all the different people it attracted, but they loved it even more during the winter. Sure, it resembled a great empire after it had collapsed during those months, only to be made great again once the weather turned, but they loved that they could spend more time getting to know the people that did visit. They also loved each other and the peace and quiet that winter provided which enabled them to spend more time as a family. They had two children, a boy and a girl, both teenagers, and the off season afforded them the time to support whatever activities they participated in. Their son starred on the basketball team. He was All Cape Cod and planned to play basketball at Stonehill College. Their daughter ran the school newspaper, with intentions of heading to school for journalism. Both worked at the hotel during the summer, making huge sums of money that they saved for college. Their parents contributed as well, and between that and an academic scholarship for the daughter and athletic money for their son, the lower middle-class family made it work. And most importantly, they were happy.

The bartender poured a drink for the girl from the front desk. From a distance, it looked to be vodka and soda with a splash of cranberry. It was possible that everything in her life needed to have some pink in it, including her drink. She nodded at Jeremy and and took a sip.

"So what are you boys doing here? Some beach time?" the waitress asked.

"Umm, it's 22 degrees outside," Jeremy answered.

"Pretty sure it was a joke," Shady interjected. "Don't mind him. He gets a little Cher-like when he doesn't eat regularly."

"Well, we better fix that then. Do you know what you want?"

"Two bacon blue burgers and a couple of Dos Equis. Amber if you have it."

"We have the Amber on draft. Tall or short?"

"Two tall boys, if he can handle it," Shady winked.

"You're a regular comedian today," Jeremy stated. "Two tall ones."

"Coming right up."

"So there are two things on my mind that I have to ask," Jeremy said once she was out of earshot.

"Fire away."

"For the last fifteen years, I've watched you follow my sister around like a lost puppy. All of a sudden, Lindsey shows up and it's as if those fifteen years never existed."

"That's not true."

"Don't get me wrong. I grant you that Lindsey's hot. I'll also grant you that my sister can be hard to deal with. And I will even grant you that most guys would be thrilled to know that their best friend wasn't interested in their sister. But you guys are perfect for each other in a really awkward, no one else could deal with either of you sort of way."

"Thanks. I think."

"I just thought we were family. All three of us."

"We are family," Shady responded. "Just more like brother-brother and brother-sister than husband-wife and brother-in-laws."

"Do you love her?"

"Your sister?"

"I know you love my sister. I meant Lindsey."

The waitress dropped off a couple of burgers and the conversation continued. It provided Shady with a much needed moment to collect his thoughts.

"Let's just say, she was a welcome distraction that I needed."

"Then what are we doing here?" Jeremy pleaded. "You're chasing after two killers and a girl you don't even love."

"Because it's the right thing to do. And maybe, I need to prove something to myself."

"Which brings me to my second question."

The waitress returned again, this time with two shot glasses of whiskey. She placed one in front of each of them. "Courtesy of the young lady at the bar."

They both raised the shots to toast the girl, and she nodded with a smile.

"You're unreal," Shady said.

"What do you mean?"

"You weren't even nice to her when we checked in!"

"Let's just say I ooze masculinity out of every pore. Can you give me a room key?"

"You're not taking her to our room," Shady stated.

"Of course not. I'm going to go to *her* room, but I need a key to get into *our* room so I don't wake you up in the middle of the night," Jeremy answered.

Shady slid the key across the table. "How considerate of you."

"I thought so."

"Just don't stay out too late. The first ferry leaves at 6:30am."

"Yes, dad."

"Brother. We're like brothers. And use a condom."

"Yes, dad."

"And don't worry. I've got the bill."

"I wasn't worried," Jeremy smiled as he wandered toward the bar.

Shady left some cash on the table and began the lonely walk along the harbor from the bar to the newer part of the hotel. He flipped through a few old movies on the TV once back in the room, before deciding that staring at the dark ceiling was a better option. Big Show had climbed onto the bed as well and the bed seemed to groan under the combined weight of them both. A couple of hours later, he heard the key unlock the door to the room, and Jeremy entered. Big Show didn't even flinch. He was some watchdog. Jeremy did his best to be quiet as he went to the bathroom and and brushed his teeth, but there was no need to be for Shady was wide awake.

"That was pretty quick," Shady said.

"You think so? We spent about 45 minutes at the bar before going back to her room, and then did it three times in an hour."

"Three   times?   That's   pretty impressive. How was it?"

"She was ok. I was spectacular."

"Congratulations."

"Everyone's got to be good at something," Jeremy answered as he climbed into his bed.

"You said earlier you had two things to ask me," Shady mentioned, "but you only asked me one. What was the other?"

Jeremy wasn't sure he wanted to have the rest of that conversation at 3:30am after having had several drinks, but he went for it anyway. "What happened in Dallas?" he blurted at last.

"You mean at my dad's funeral?"

"No," Jeremy shook his head. "When you used to live there. I know you were a cop. I've read all the stories."

"Oh. That. Well, if you've read all the stories, then you know."

"But I want to know from your perspective."

"Believe me. I ask myself the same question every day. I was on patrol with my partner. Typical day. There was this convenience store that had been owned by the same couple for the last 50 years, and we were in there getting a Slim Jim and a coffee when these two kids walked in. Maybe 20 years old. One of them demanded money from the guy at the cash register and pulled out a gun. His wife started screaming so the guy backhanded her across the room. The husband then stopped putting money in the bag and ran over to her. The robber got pissed and knocked him unconscious with the butt end of his gun. Blood everywhere. When I saw that, something inside me snapped. I charged at the one guy, drove him into the other and lifted us all through the plate glass window. When we landed, my partner dragged one of them away, and I just started pummeling the other. It took three cops to pull me off him. The kid slipped into a coma for two months. He recovered eventually, but it was a long road back and from what I hear he was never quite the same. I was investigated by the police and convicted by the media and in the court of public opinion because the kid was African American."

"But you didn't mean to hurt him that badly."

"At that moment I did. Turns out he hit his head when we landed and that's what caused the problem. Nothing I could have really done about that. I'm sure pummeling him didn't help either. But I can say in all honesty that race had nothing to do with it. Hell, my partner was African American. If the couple was African American and the criminals were white, I would have done the same thing. I just couldn't stand someone abusing the elderly. That guy would have probably given the kid the money if he had only asked."

"What happened with the police investigation? The articles don't really say."

"After the fact, I was found not guilty, but in order to save my parents the grief and harassment, I resigned in the middle of it all and moved away. Next stop, Niantic."

"Didn't people realize you might have stopped that kid from killing the owner?"

"I'm not sure. But I didn't like how angry I got. So I thought it'd be a good idea if I didn't put myself in that situation again."

"And so this is about..."

"I was a good cop. And I liked helping people. I guess maybe I want to see if I can still do it."

Big Show crawled toward the top of the bed and laid his head down across Shady's chest. He sensed his sadness.

Jeremy nodded. It all finally made sense. The mystery that was Shady's life. His never ending desire to help people. And the inherent sadness that had come with losing the one thing that gave his life a purpose. But Dallas's loss was Niantic's gain. *When one life ends, another begins.*

XIV ~The Untold Tale~

Most days, Shady woke up fifteen minutes before his alarm did. It was a reflex he had learned in the police academy where 30 seconds late was treated the same as 30 minutes. He was that rare person who could go from sound asleep to wide awake in seconds flat.

He poured his first cup of coffee into a thermos and headed to the station where he was regularly the first officer to arrive for roll call. They loved him at the Southwest Dallas station. He was big, strong, smart and had the respect of both his fellow officers as well as the citizens in his precinct. It might not have been the career his father envisioned for him when he was growing up, but it didn't take his dad long to see that it was a great fit. Shady glowed every time he slipped on his uniform. He loved what it stood for and what he stood for when he was wearing it.

His partner came from a police family. Will Johnson's father, uncle, and both of his brothers were all Dallas police officers. Will and Shady came through the academy as two of the most decorated officers in years. Together, they were an amazing pair, working to make the streets of Southwest Dallas a safer place to live. Will was one of their own. He had grown up in the area they patrolled, but Shady had been accepted as one of their own by association with Will. Shady loved working there as opposed to the town he grew up in, where the job would have been so bland, that the average shift would have involved a few cups of coffee, a couple of parking tickets and a traffic citation for jaywalking. Southwest Dallas wasn't the toughest area in the city, but it was definitely in the top 10.

On most days, Shady drove while Will rode shotgun in their cruiser. There was no real reason for it. It was just something they did on day one and continued with every day for the next five years. There were two things to note about cops. The first is that they were superstitious. If they didn't get shot on the first day while doing something, they weren't about to tempt fate after that, even if what they were doing really had nothing to do with it. If you believed you were safe because you drove, or because you didn't drive, then you were.

They were cruising along, not really looking for anything when they approached a stop light. Shady had braked slightly when he saw the yellow light in the other direction, since he knew it was about to turn green. Turned out that slight tap of the brakes probably saved an ugly collision as a car whipped through the intersection from the right without the slightest of hesitation. If anything, it had sped up.

Shady flipped on the siren and made a cautious, yet expeditious left turn through the intersection. They caught up to the car about a half mile down the road.

"Looks like a young female driver," Will said.

Shady punched the license plate number into their computer.

"Jillian Thomas. 22. Cedar Hill," Shady answered. "No points on her license."

They approached the car calmly, Will on the passenger side, Shady on the driver's. She didn't look as though she was going to cause much trouble. Well, maybe a different kind of trouble, Will thought as he noticed her unbutton her blouse a couple of buttons revealing ample cleavage.

"Ma'am. Do you know why we pulled you over?" Shady asked.

"I know. I'm really sorry," the girl blurted out. "The light turned yellow just as I was approaching it. I tapped the brakes, but I didn't think I could stop on time so I went on through."

"It actually looked more like you sped up to be honest," Shady answered in a tone that was both friendly but assertive.

"Oh, I didn't mean to," she smiled, leaning forward a bit, trying to get Shady's attention. His eyes remained fixated on her forehead. Will's never drifted north of her neckline. "I'm just running really late for my Psychology midterm."

"You're a student?"

"Yes. At SMU. And my professor is a big stickler about being on time. Is there *anything* I could do?"

"As a matter of fact there is. Learn that yellow means slow down, not speed up, and that the brake pedal is the one on the left," Shady answered as he tore off a ticket and handed it to her.

"But I've never gotten a ticket before," she pleaded.

"Well, I'm not trying to make history here, but you could have caused a serious accident. Have a nice day."

"Great," she mumbled under her breath. "300 cops in Southwest Dallas and I get the only gay one."

Shady heard her comment and chuckled to himself as he walked away.

"I could have never given her a ticket," Will said as they climbed back into the cruiser.

"Why not? She almost t-boned us."

"Did you see her cleavage?"

"Of course I saw it. Just because I'm professional, doesn't mean I'm blind."

"I would have just waited to find some fat, slob guy with a broken tail light to hit quota."

"And that's why I'm driving and you're not," Shady laughed. "Lud's?"

"Of course."

The second thing to note about cops was that they liked their routines. They liked to do the same thing at the same time every day and when something disrupted it, they believed it threw their karma off. Funny thing about criminals. They knew that cops liked their routines and they counted on that. On a normal day, Will and Shady would have arrived at the Ludkevic Deli by 9:00am, but today they were late. Will was grabbing their coffees in the back, while Shady decided between a Nacho and Tabasco flavored Monster Slim Jim in an aisle near the front. Two men walked in. Boys really. They couldn't have been much more than 19. One stayed by the window, blocking the view from the outside. The other took a quick look around and saw no one else in the store. He pulled a .45 caliber handgun from his waistband and pointed it at the store owner's head.

"Empty the drawer! Put it in a paper bag!"

The owner's wife screamed. More of a shriek really. The gunman backhanded her into the Hostess Cupcake stand, where she laid in a crumpled heap. Her husband stopped putting cash in the bag and ran over to her. The gunman was enraged. He pointed the gun at them both before smashing the man on the top of his head with the butt end of the .45. The man was bleeding and unconscious on the ground next to his wife.

With his gun still pointed at the couple, the robber turned ever so slightly to grab the paper bag on the counter. It was just enough time for Shady to make his move. He came charging down the aisle and lowered his shoulder as he had done a thousand times before on the gridiron. Shady lifted the man into the air and drove him up and into the second man, and through the plate glass window of the store front. The three men landed in a pile of shattered glass as people in the street scattered.

Will raced from the back of the store and dragged one of the robbers through the shrouds of broken glass and cuffed him. Shady reared back with his catcher's mitt sized hand and began pummeling the other one's face with sledgehammer-like blows. Repeatedly. One after the other. Three other officers had now ascended onto the scene and it took all of them to pull Shady off the man. His muscles flexing, his face taut with rage, Shady didn't even realize at that moment he had been shot. The entire scene had unfolded in less than twenty seconds.

A half-ripped paper bag lay on the sidewalk. Thirty-two dollars had fallen out of it.

XV ~*The Search Unfolds*~

The slow ferry to Nantucket that was packed during the summer as people sought to escape from their everyday problems for a while, was nearly empty in January. The holidays were over. The weather was cold, damp and dreary. And much of the island was shut down until spring.

They climbed the metal staircase from the car port and entered the main cabin.

"Want to sit outside?" Shady asked with a smile, pointing to the ice covered benches.

"Umm, no. But I could go for a coffee."

They took their cups of coffee and a couple of sausage, egg and cheese sandwiches that had been heated far too long in the microwave and sat in a booth in the mostly empty cabin.

"What makes you so sure they're out here?" Jeremy asked before adding, "God, these things are awful. And hot!"

He spat part of it back into the wrapper much to Shady's amusement.

"Because Mexico is too far for them to go without getting caught. And even though

Canada is close, our countries have too good of a relationship. They'd get stopped at the border. So they have two choices. Hide out somewhere until the search dies down. Or try to sneak into Canada through an unusual channel. And what better place to do either of those things from than a nearly deserted northern island in the middle of the Atlantic?"

Jeremy nodded. What he said made sense. A little more than two hours later, the ferry began to dock in the harbor of the Grey Lady. It was an unusually sunny day in January. Clear blue skies, but cold. The grey shake shingle homes were covered in a coating of ice and glistened in the sunlight.

They drove off the ferry and toward the cobblestone streets of the town center. During the summer, there was nary a parking space to be had. In January, you could take your pick. They walked into The Fog Island Cafe and immediately felt all eyes upon them as if they had just come in off the water and invaded Normandy. The place was packed with locals that all knew each other.

"So what's the plan?" Jeremy asked once they were seated in a side booth. "Look for the truck?"

"The truck isn't here."

"How do you know that?"

"Had a hunch that was confirmed by a friend this morning. No record of it on the ferry for the last two days. And...they found the truck in a parking lot in Hyannis. If you think about it, it makes sense. The car ferry is the only way to track someone who goes to the island. If they just walked on and paid cash, there would be no record of them."

"But what if they went to the Vineyard instead?"

Shady looked as though he hadn't considered that possibility and didn't really want to consider it now. "Why you gotta crap in my cornflakes?" he answered.

"I'm just sayin..."

"The Vineyard is bigger and more commercial. If you want to disappear, the Grey Lady is where you go." Shady seemed to be trying to convince himself of that now.

"Ok, let's say you're right. How do we find them?"

"Well, they're not going to stay in a hotel. That's for certain. They probably broke into a vacant house in one of the more remote areas of the island. Most likely one with a car because the The Wave doesn't run during the off season."

"What the heck is The Wave?"

"The busing system that takes you all over the island."

"So we need to find a remote house with a car. Shouldn't be that difficult. Should probably only take about three weeks," Jeremy chided.

"Don't worry. I've got a plan. Wherever they are, what's the one thing they'll need?" Shady asked.

Jeremy thought it over. He was thinking like a cop now. "Food?"

"Exactly. Which is why I'm going to drop you off at Stop & Shop."

"And what are you going to be doing?"

"I'm going to be searching the island. Starting with the three most remote areas. Madaket. Tom Nevers. And Polpis."

He only found four houses in all of Madaket that had a car in the driveway, and one of them was occupied by an older couple back from lunch. They waved when they saw him and he pretended to be out for a walk.

"Brave man!" the older gentleman shouted.

"It's a bit chilly for sure," Shady answered. "Not many of us on the streets at this time of year."

"Not many people on the island *period* at this time of year."

"I sure haven't seen many."

"Only one other sign of life on this side of the island. House at the end of the cul de sac. Haven't seen any actual people, but I've seen a car a couple of times."

"Well, enjoy the peace and quiet while it lasts," Shady smiled.

"You too."

Shady decided to forgo his car so as not to draw suspicion and walked to the end of the street. The house was pretty secluded with tall hedges on three sides and conservation land on the fourth. Shady didn't see a car in the driveway so he decided to explore a little deeper. He walked around back of the grey, shake shingle home that looked just like every other one on the island and peered in through the patio doors. Someone was clearly living there. A few dishes were in the sink. The coffee pot was half full. And there were clothes and bags strewn across the living room.

Shady pulled a Swiss Army knife from his jacket pocket and flipped the latch to a bedroom window. He climbed through it as delicately as a man his size could, landing not so gently on the floor.

He examined the clothes in the living room a bit more closely. Mostly men's clothes, but some women's as well. He was holding a bra by its straps when he felt a set of eyes on him. A man was staring at Shady from the doorway, before bolting out of the house and into the yard — with Shady in hot pursuit.

Shady caught up to him mere feet from the road and leapt into the air. He planted his shoulder into the man's back and drove him headfirst into the crushed white sea shell driveway.

"Where is she?!" Shady growled.

"Who??"

"Lindsey."

"I have no idea who that is."

Shady flipped him not so gently onto his back like a fisherman preparing to gut their catch. With his one hand pressing on the man's chest to hold him down, he pulled out the picture of the prisoners. He looked at the picture and then at the man. Decided the man wasn't either of them.

"Who are you and why did you run?" Shady asked.

"Because I thought you were robbing me. I'm no hero. I'm just a guy working his tail off for 50K a year," the man explained.

"Then how are you affording that house?"

"Well, that's the thing..."

"You're squatting?"

"We prefer the term unauthorized house sitting. Are you going to call the cops?"

"That depends."

"On what?"

"On if you help me find the people I'm looking for."

"I'd be more than happy to do that, but do you think you can get off of me first? You're crushing my solar plexus."

XVI ~The Chicken Box~

Shady pulled up in front of the Super Stop & Shop and threw open the door to the truck for Jeremy. "Get in," he told him.

"Did you find them?" he asked as he climbed in.

"Not yet, but we know they're here."

"How do you know that?"

"Because a new friend told me they're staying in Tom Nevers. Meet Joe."

Joe reached over the front bench of the truck to shake Jeremy's hand. Jeremy shook it tentatively, not quite sure he followed what was happening.

"Joe has lived year round on the island for 30 years. Knows everybody here and one of his boys said he saw three people matching the description of Lindsey and the two prisoners yesterday."

"Great. Let's bring 'em in," Jeremy said eagerly.

"We don't know exactly where they are right now, but we know the house they're staying in."

"What if they're back on the run?"

"We have people at the ferry, harbor and airport. If they show at any of those places, we'll know about it. I don't think they'll be suspicious. The news says the feds are following leads down in Georgia. They think they're headed for the Mexican border."

"So what are we going to do?"

"We're going to go to The Chicken Box and wait for them to return to the house. It's right down the street."

"We're going to a farm?"

"It's a bar."

"And it's got a great beer selection," Joe added.

Jeremy shrugged. He supposed that was as good a place as any to wait.

The Chicken Box had been a Nantucket staple for more than 50 years. It started as a restaurant and bar that attracted blues musicians from New York, before gradually transitioning to just a bar without food and eventually expanding to include other musical acts from reggae to country and rock. The bar was the east coast version of the Whiskey a Go-Go, igniting the careers of soon to be stars, reigniting the careers of once-were stars, and providing a place for current popular acts to get away for a nice weekend and get back to their roots by playing a small venue.

A long bar, pool table, shuffleboard and multiple dartboards attracted the locals even when there wasn't music. It was a no frills, relaxed place, on an island that didn't have many of them, where you could drink a beer out of the bottle.

The three of them bellied up to the bar and ordered a round of drinks. Big Show laid at Shady's feet.

"Whale's Tale," Shady nodded to the bartender.

"Same," Joe followed.

"I'll have a Corona," Jeremy said.

Shady and Joe simultaneously turned their heads as if to say, *are you serious?*

"What?"

"Nothing says tourist quite like a Corona," Shady responded.

"I like Corona. And I have no idea what a Whale's Tale is."

"It's a local IPA."

"Fine. Make it 3."

"You want an umbrella with yours?" Shady asked when the bartender placed the bottles in front of them.

"Funny," Jeremy grumbled while they all enjoyed a chuckle at his expense.

Not five minutes later, two men walked in and sat a few seats down from them. Big Show sprang up at attention and let out a deep "*Whoof.*" The men looked strangely familiar, but Jeremy couldn't quite place them. Until he could. Their hair colors were different and one of them was clean shaven while the other sported a goatee now instead of a full beard, but they were definitely the men they were looking for. He went to elbow Shady, and came up with nothing but air as Shady had already made his way to the end of the bar.

"You looked better with a beard," Shady told the one man.

"Do I know you?" Bates Carideo growled without even looking up.

"No. You don't. Where's the girl?"

The words had just left his mouth when Lindsey appeared around the corner from the ladies room. "Shady," she said, sounding surprised before she noticed her dog. "Big Show? Hey buddy!"

But the dog didn't leave Shady's side. He sat at attention, protecting his new King.

"You know this guy?" Bones Smith asked. "How'd you find us?"

"It wasn't that difficult. Just had to think like a criminal."

Bones rose to his feet. He wasn't a small man, but he seemed like he was standing in front of Shady. "Listen, big man. This isn't your business."

"You made it my business when you kidnapped someone I cared about," Shady responded. When Bones reached for his pocket, Shady grabbed a nearby barstool with both hands and jabbed him in the stomach with the end of the seatback. As he doubled over in pain, Shady swung the chair violently upward smashing him on the underside of his chin, knocking him ass backwards to the floor.

Bates grabbed a bottle from the bar and went to smash it over Shady's head, but Shady was too quick and too strong for him. He caught Bone's arm midair and slammed it off the bar until the bottle fell harmlessly to the floor. He followed with a thunderous backhand that sent Bates flying across several barstools that splintered upon impact.

"Who are you?" Bates mumbled.

Jeremy stood over the man. "He's Shady Bad-Ass-o, bitch!"

"Let's just say when you're planning a prison break, you should always prepare for something unexpected," Shady advised. "A variable if you will. I'm the variable."

"Don't...move!" Bones shouted. He had a gun against Lindsey's temple. He was shaking.

It took a fraction of a second for Shady to draw his own gun and point it back at Bones.

"Drop it!" Bones ordered.

"Do the math, Bonesy. Or are you Batesey? Either way, there's only one scenario where you leave here alive. If you kill her, you'll be dead one second later. If you try to kill me, you'll be dead. Only way you live is if you let her go."

"If I let her go, I'll be headed back to prison for life. And that's the same as being dead."

"He's not going to hurt her," a familiar female voice interjected from behind them both.

"Casey?" Shady answered, puzzled.

"How'd you find us?" Jeremy asked.

"Tracking device on your phone. I pay your bills, remember? They're together, Shady. They've been together for years."

"She's lying," Lindsey pleaded.

"I saw pictures of her in court at his trial."

"Drop...the gun!" Bones repeated. "Last chance."

Shady shook his head. "Nah," he said before firing a bullet into Bones' knee. The bullet shattered his kneecap instantly and he crumpled to the ground in a heap. Lindsey ran over to Shady and threw her arms around him. Casey looked disappointed. Jeremy kicked Bones' gun across the floor and pushed him to the ground, while Joe and a couple of locals held Bates down.

"Can I talk to you a minute privately?" Shady asked.

Lindsey nodded and they stepped outside the back door, out of ear shot from everyone else, but sirens could be heard from Nantucket's small police force as they ascended on The Chicken Box.

"I know you were with him," Shady asserted.

"Of course I was with him. They kidnapped me," Lindsey answered, reaching for Shady's hand, only to have him pull it away.

"Went to Kansas for a guy? You got me to fix the old truck and you probably drove it down to Baltimore when I was out of town and left it there as there as the switch car. Then took the train back."

She looked like she wanted to argue the point, before coming to the realization it was pointless to do so. He knew.

"Like I said, I know you're with him. What I don't know is why you were with me?"

"If you really believe that, why'd you come after me then?"

"I guess I wanted to hear you admit it to my face," he answered.

She hesitated for a minute before deciding to tell the truth for the first time in a long time. "When I met you, yes, at first it was something to do in a boring, little shit kicker town. But then I fell for you. I really cared for you, Shady. I still do."

"And yet you left with him."

"I didn't know he was going to break out."

"Give me a break. You moved into the town where the prison was."

"Yeah, so I could visit him. I was just being nice. But I never thought he was ever going to get out. And then when he did, what was I supposed to do?"

"The right thing," Shady answered plainly.

"What now?" she asked.

"The cops are inside."

She bowed her head and nodded.

"Which is why I'd go that way," he continued, pointing in the opposite direction. "The last ferry of the night is leaving in 15 minutes. My truck is parked on the side of the building. If you leave now, you just might make it."

She hugged him tightly and kissed him softly on the cheek. "I'm sorry. I'm *so* sorry."

"You've got a second chance at a second chance. Make something of your life this time. You have too much potential not to."

As he watched her walk rapidly away, her best feature didn't look quite as seductive anymore. The cops would probably go after her for a while. But she was smart and resourceful. Eventually, he figured they'd stop looking. After all, thanks to Shady, they had the ones they really wanted. Stone-faced and sad, Shady walked back inside just in time to see

John *Bates* Carideo and Steve *Bones* Smith being escorted out the door. Neither was walking.

"Where's the girl?" the police Sergeant asked.

"She wasn't with them," Shady answered to Jeremy and Casey's bewilderment. "They cut her loose somewhere on the Cape. I guess she was slowing them down."

"Then where is she now?"

"I have no idea."

"She aided and abetted two murderers. We need to bring her in."

"I wouldn't know anything about that," Shady said. "So unless you need me for something, I'm going home."

XVII ~Aftermath~

Casey burst through the front door of Shady's house without waiting for an invitation. She found him folding clothes in the bedroom.

"What the hell, Shady? What the hell?"

"What's your problem?"

"My problem is that you let the girlfriend of a convicted murderer go free."

"She didn't kill anyone."

"She helped them escape! She's not the person you think she is."

"Do you really think I don't know this? She told me she followed a guy to Kansas. I read all the same articles you did. And when I walked through her house with the cops the day they escaped, the first thing I noticed was that all of her favorite outfits were missing. If you're kidnapping someone, you don't wait around for them to pick out their favorite clothes."

"Of course you'd know her favorite outfits."

"What's that supposed to mean?"

"Nothing. But if you knew all that, then why'd you go after her?"

"Because I knew the feds would screw it up. And because I had something to prove to myself."

"About being a cop? I know what happened in Dallas. Well, at least I know what I read."

He stopped folding clothes for the first time and looked up at her. "How long have you known?" he asked.

"A couple of years."

"How come you never said anything?"

"I figured you'd tell me if you wanted to."

He shook his head. "I've gone over it in my mind a thousand times. I'm certainly not proud of my behavior, but I also can't explain it either."

He took some of his folded clothes and started placing them in a duffle bag.

"Where are you going?"

"You remember my high school friend that was sick?"

"Yes."

"She passed away last night. The last time I saw her, she made me promise I'd give her eulogy and I have no idea what to say."

"Just speak from the heart and you'll be fine."

"That's just it. She doesn't want something heartfelt. In fact, she wants the exact opposite of heartfelt."

He zipped the bag closed and grabbed his wedding and death suit from the closet.

"Can I ask you something?" Casey asked.

"Sure."

"Did you love her?"

"My friend?"

Casey shook her head. "Lindsey."

"I liked her," he answered in a measured tone.

"What was it about her? And if you tell me it's because she was hot, I'm going to punch you straight in the face."

Shady fought back a slight grin and for one fleeting moment contemplated saying exactly that, but as John Keating said in Dead Poets Society, *there was a time for daring and a time for caution and the wise man knew which was called for.* "Let's just say that after following you around like a lost puppy for the last fifteen years, she was a welcome distraction."

"Enough of a distraction to sleep with her?"

"Is that a question or a statement?"

"Maybe both."

"I plead the fifth."

"And a distraction from what?" Casey demanded to know.

"A distraction from how much I loved you," he answered, surprised at how easily the words had come out.

"All this time and you never even asked me out for an actual date."

"Because you never left the door open even a crack—until Lindsey appeared."

"So let me get this straight. You loved me so much that you slept with another woman? That's the story you're going with?"

"It's not sexy, but it's the truth," Shady shrugged, before adding, "Your brother said he would look after The Big Show for me while I was gone, but he's a bit of a flake. Do you think you could look in on him?"

"Of course."

Casey stood on the top step of the porch with Big Show sitting at attention by her side as Shady's truck pulled down the driveway and out of view. The dog leaned up against her and nudged her hand with his nose. She smiled and reached down to run one hand along the underside of his neck while the other scratched behind his ear.

"Yeah, I like him too," she said.

XVIII ~Controlled Irreverence~

Shady looked out across the church pews, cleared his throat and took a sip of water. "It's really nice to see so many familiar faces today. In case you are wondering who I am and why I am giving the eulogy, my name is Sal Badissimo and Lisa and I were very good friends in high school. As often happens, we lost touch over the years and I've never been on those crazy sites Snaptalk or Instapic or whatever they're called, where I hear everyone posts pictures of their dogs wearing sunglasses, their one year old's birthday party and vacation pictures of places that the rest of us will probably never have the opportunity to visit. But Lisa and I were reunited a few weeks back when my father passed away. It was then that she made me promise to do this, although I'm not exactly sure why. First of all, let's just call it as it is. There is nothing courageous or graceful about dying of Cancer. If there are any research doctors here today, get to work, because this disease does not discriminate. It doesn't care if you drank and smoked your entire life, or ate nothing but fruits and vegetables. So for those of you expecting me to talk about how courageous her fight against Cancer was, and how graceful she was at the end, this is not going to be that eulogy.

Lisa was a straight shooter. If you didn't want an honest answer, you didn't ask the question," Shady began to laughter throughout the church. "She hated weathermen, politicians and Roger Goodell. Basically, she hated anyone who was constantly wrong.

She couldn't stand mothers whose hair and makeup were perfect at 7:00am. *"Did they wake up at 5:00am to do it?"* she would ask.

She didn't trust anyone who shopped at Trader Joe's, and she always sent her kids to school bake sales with store bought cookies from Kroger's instead of baking them herself.

She hated reality TV. *Too many stupid people all assembled in one place is never a good idea. Besides, how real is it really when they stage most of it anyway?*

She thought that parents who let their sons wear big baggy clothes, and baseball hats with flat brims and the stickers still on them, and parents who let their daughters dress like pole dancers and high class call girls should be visited by DCF.

Similarly, she thought that parents who lived vicariously through their children's athletic careers, should be lined up and shot. *A fat, out of shape, non-athlete, rarely produces a great athlete. It's their fault. They gave their kid bad genes. Not the coach's. And certainly not the kid's. Some kids just stink. Deal with it.*

But she was also far from perfect herself. She once made out with her best friend's boyfriend after having a bit too much to drink. She didn't throw a birthday party for her two year old, because *she won't remember it anyway.* And she forgot her wedding anniversary — twice.

Lisa was however, smart, funny and loyal in a world where most people struggled to even be one of those three. She was a wife, mother and friend and how good she was at all three of those probably depended on your perspective. And she couldn't have cared less what you thought. That's what I loved about her. If she didn't like you, and you're here today, she wouldn't have second thoughts and think that maybe she had judged you too harshly. She'd hope you tripped down the steps on the way out. And that's what I'll miss most about her. She was a genuine article, one that comes along once in a generation. And she was my friend."

As Shady made his way to towards Lisa's family in the front pew, her husband intercepted him with a hug.

"I hope it was ok," Shady said softly.

"It was better than ok. It was perfect."

The Priest seemed to have a slightly different view of the eulogy as he awkwardly stepped forward. Shady took his seat, and he couldn't help but wonder how many in attendance were now worried about taking a wrong step when they exited the church. Lisa would have definitely approved.

Everyone stood and Shady did so with his arms and hands straight by his sides. Suddenly, another hand reached inside his. It was smaller, more delicate, and fit perfectly inside Shady's enormous catcher's mitt sized palm. He was surprised to find Casey looking up at him with a smile.

"I decided to open the door a crack. I hope that's ok," she whispered.

"It's better than ok. It's perfect," he answered as he closed his fingers tightly around hers.

When one life ends, another begins. Shady was home at last.

Author's Notes

The Untold Tale of Shady Badesso has been two years in the writing. While it touches on many of the same elements and themes as my other works—friendship, love and loyalty—it also incorporates something new for me. A little bit of suspense. As are all of my novels, the story is set in my adopted home state of Connecticut, a place I have now lived for more than twenty years. What made this story even more fun to write is that I was also able to sprinkle in a trip to my wife's and my favorite place to visit in the entire world—Nantucket, a beautiful island off the coast of Cape Cod that we spend some time in each summer.

At its core, *Shady Badesso* is a story of redemption, as one man attempts to come to terms with the worst thing he has ever done, while spending his life trying to make amends for it. The battle within the main character is whether he can ever forgive himself or even whether he needs to be forgiven at all.

On a side note, the names of the villains and the female lead are actually two former students of mine and a former soccer player who won a naming contest I had held. The students were those unmotivated ones that you still couldn't help but love. They made coming to school entertaining and worthwhile, and it's been fun to see the people they've become (through Facebook). Real-life Casey is a wonderful girl from a wonderful family, every bit as charming as the character in the book. This story is for all three of them.

Enjoy this story? Turn the page for a glimpse at another novel by Matt Micros, *Slow Drinkers, Giant Ballbags & Smelly Bastards*...

"Jim Reilly woke up dead and was really pissed off about it. He snapped open the paper while sitting on the can, the way he did every morning, and found himself staring at an old picture of himself in the obituary section on Page 6. It wasn't even a good picture."

With the Irish Wake just three days away, his best friend convinces him to play along so they can find out who is responsible for the sick joke. The resulting chaos sees Jim reunited with old friends, acquaintances and family members – most of whom he hasn't seen since his wife passed away three years earlier. Fueled by his frustration, Jim takes us on an unexpected and unintentional laugh riot journey through a cast of characters that include slow drinkers, giant ballbags and smelly bastards. A story that is as sure to tug at your heart as give you a belly laugh, Jim finds that it took dying, to actually bring him back to life.

SLOW DRINKERS, GIANT BALLBAGS & SMELLY BASTARDS

I THE END

Jim Reilly woke up dead and he was really pissed off about it. He snapped open the paper while sitting on the can, the way he did every morning, and found himself staring at an old picture of himself in the obituary section on Page 6. It wasn't even a good picture.

"Jim Reilly, 45, of Stratford, died suddenly yesterday of unknown causes. A lifelong sports enthusiast, Jim was a New York Mets season ticket holder for 15 years in the seats directly in front of Jerry Seinfeld's suite. They spoke five times during the games they attended together, but he believed they had an unspoken mutual admiration, even though there was no logical reason to believe that. Jim was a novelist in his free time, when he wasn't working for the Town of Stratford in their Park and Rec Department as a youth league coordinator. His books had sold a grand total of 42 copies, when he decided to take matters into his own hands and buy a few hundred copies, which drove him high enough up the

Amazon Best Seller Lists to get recognized by people who would not have otherwise seen him. The response was nothing short of amazing, as he went on to slowly grow a following that helped him sell two million copies over the next year. And yet, he never moved out of the small home he had shared with his wife of twenty years, the pre-deceased, Sharon.

Jim believed in accountability instead of excuses, kicking off from the 25 yard line, paying people exactly what they were worth regardless of the demand, and he was vehemently opposed to baseball managers removing a good player from a game due to a righty-lefty match up. He also believed that he could do nearly any job in the country better than anyone who currently did them, and had no problem sharing his ideas with anyone who would listen--along with a few who would have preferred not to.

He is survived by a brother, Sam, whose whereabouts is unknown, and millions of fans spread around the globe, who are encouraged to attend the funeral service, as no one should be buried alone. In lieu of traditional calling hours, there will be an Irish Wake held at Finnegan's Pub in New Haven on Saturday night from 5:00pm til close."

"What the hell?!" Jim groused, as he quickly folded the paper back up and reached for his cell phone.

He called the contact number on the inside of the paper. Someone answered on the 5th ring.

"Obits and op-eds," the voice said.

"Hello. This is Jim Reilly calling. This morning, you guys ran an obituary for me, but as you can hear, it was a bit pre-mature. I'm clearly not dead."

"Interesting. Well, we just run what people give us to run," the man responded.

"Who gave it to you? It had to be submitted online. You should be able to trace the payment or server," Jim insisted.

"Let me have a look. What was the name again?"

"Jim Reilly. James Reilly."

"Forty-five years old from Stratford?"

"Yes."

"It says here it was actually dropped off in person along with the payment."

"But who paid?"

"That it doesn't say. Paid in cash apparently."

"Cash?? Who pays in cash these days?" Jim asked.

"Apparently this person did."

"Well, you need to write a retraction."

"I'm not sure we do retractions."

"What do you mean you don't do retractions?"

"We've never had someone come back from the dead before."

"I was never dead. Someone is obviously playing some sort of sick joke."

"I suppose if you can get us proof you are alive, we might be able to get something in next week."

"Next *week*?? People will be upset. Some might even be hysterical. You need to take care of this straight away."

"Let me talk to my boss. This is a bit unusual. Not sure what we would call it. Obituary comes from the Latin word, obit, which means death."

"Call it a Vitauary then. From the Latin word for life! Just get this sorted!" Jim huffed as he hung up.

He immediately dialed another number.

"Aaron Harrington," the voice on the other end answered.

"It's Jim. What are you up to?"

"I'm at work," Aaron said, sounding puzzled.

"Can you break away?"

"I suppose so. Is everything ok?"

"No. But I'll explain when I see you. Let's meet at the Sitting Duck in 20 minutes," Jim said.

The bar was a local watering hole whose clientele hadn't changed much in the past 20 years. Dark, not necessarily dingy, but not immaculate either. Jim grabbed a table near the back of the bar and ordered a Guinness while he waited for Aaron. It was a bit early for a drink, but surely if there was an occasion that warranted it, it had to be your death. He skipped the customary greetings when Aaron arrived, opting instead to shove the paper in his face and point to the article in question. "Read this."

"Well, hello!" Aaron exclaimed. "Haven't spoken to you in weeks. Haven't seen you in months, but let's skip the pleasantries and shove a paper in my face."

"Just read it," Jim insisted.

Aaron glanced at it casually at first, before a bemused look overtook his face as he read on. "Is this some kind of joke?"

"You tell me," Jim answered.

"Whoever wrote this has you pegged pretty spot on," Aaron laughed.

"What do you mean?"

"Just mean that whoever wrote it must know you pretty well. So who did write it?"

"I have no idea. The person paid cash and dropped it off in person. And the paper is saying it could take a few days to get a retraction in."

"Well, I wouldn't worry too much about it. After all, you are alive. And I don't think most people our age tend to scour the obits on a daily basis. We're not 90."

"It only takes one," Jim insisted. "Then they tell someone, who tells someone else. With social media the way it is these days, the news could already be everywhere, and I don't want people wasting money flying clear across the country to attend my funeral."

"People don't fly across the country to attend a wake or funeral. They send flowers. But you might want to try and reach your brother just in case."

"Should we post something on Facebook?" Jim asked.

"Like what? I'm not dead?" Aaron laughed.

"Well, yeah."

"Look, I think you're looking at this all wrong," Aaron said. "You've got the opportunity to attend your own funeral. While you're alive no less. How cool is that?"

Jim appeared to be thinking about that. It was an intriguing concept. "What if no one showed up? That would be pretty embarrassing."

"I wouldn't rule that out as a possibility," Aaron said. "You have been kind of a salty recluse for the past few years. "Don't get me wrong," he quickly added when he saw Jim's face turn sour, "I understand why."

"I have not been a salty recluse," Jim responded defensively.

"You don't go anywhere. You don't do anything. You haven't written a word since she passed away.

"She was my wife. And the love of my life."

"I get that, but she was my sister and I loved her too. And I *know* she wouldn't have wanted us wallowing in misery at her leaving us. If you're honest with yourself, you know that too."

When Jim didn't respond, Aaron took that as a small victory.

"Tell you what," Aaron said, "I'll make some calls to see what I can find out. You should call your brother. And let's plan to go to this wake."

"I'm not going to the wake. That's creepy."

"It's the least you could do for the people that show up."

"I didn't invite them. I didn't tell anyone I was dead. I don't owe them anything."

Not taking "no" for an answer, Aaron said, "I'll pick you up Friday at 4:15 so we can get a table in the balcony. It's good to see you out and about."

Jim watched his brother-in-law leave while slowly sipping his Guinness. He touched the name "Sam" under his list of contacts and held the phone to his ear. After the 4th ring, Sam's voicemail picked up.

"You've reached Sam. Unfortunately, I can't get to the phone right now because I'm probably scaling Mt Everest, bungy jumping in the Everglades, whale watching in Cabo or some other crazy shit like that."

But instead of a BEEP that would allow Jim to leave a message, the voice message said the voice mail was "full" and "could not accept any messages."

He pressed the red button to end the call and continued to slowly drink his beer.